AmBITCHous

SCERINA ELIZABETH
RAJA SAVAGE

CHAPTER 1

Eva

I have no idea what fresh hell awaits me at the office as I go about my normal routine. This is carpool morning, and I'm already running late and still waiting for two of my kids.

"Roberto! Zabeth! I'm leaving in less than five minutes! I have a carpool and I already got texts from two other mothers threatening to take over if I don't arrive for their kids soon!"

As tempted as I am to let that happen, I promised myself I would not be *that* mother who's irresponsible and unreliable.

"Mom! I need five more minutes to get my 'fit together!" Zabeth shouts.

Lord have mercy with this one! She's only fifteen and already acts like a total diva, where the world as she knows it waits on her hand and foot. Thank God Roberto Jr. isn't so high maintenance. Then again, boys never are. They're so easy, as they only have one thing on their minds at this age—girls—and my son is no different.

Although he also has school studies and the soccer team on his mind as well, girls never take the back seat in his priorities. But I cannot complain because he does well in school, even with every teenage girl chasing after him. He's the school soccer star and that alone has every girl hot on his tracks to be his girlfriend. But he has no interest in being tied down by dating. No, his focus is soccer and school studies.

Five minutes later, my daughter still has yet to come down. I'm seriously tempted to leave without her. It wouldn't be the first nor the last time either.

"Zabeth!" I shout with my keys in my hand and Roberto waiting by the door for us. "IF YOU ARE NOT DOWN HERE IN ZERO-POINT-FIVE SECONDS, I AM LEAVING WITHOUT YOU!"

A moment later, she appears, taking her sweet time coming down the stairs, looking in the mirror as she applies her lipstick. A bold shade of red. Too red, perhaps, but I don't have time to argue or fight.

"It's about time!" I say as we hurry toward the door to the garage.

By the time we leave the yard, another mother has taken over the carpool since I'm running late—my friend, Helena Swan. She offered to pick Zabeth up so that I could get on with my morning. I should have let her, but knowing my daughter, I kindly declined. Zabeth would have taken advantage of me being out of the house to take even longer and hold up the carpool, which wouldn't be fair to the other children or Helena.

By the time I get the kids off to school, it's already a quarter to nine. I'm supposed to be in the office at 8:30, but maybe it's a good thing I'm not on time. As I pull near, I find pure chaos and mayhem outside of the building. Cops and ambulances are all over the place. The building is sealed off and it looks like a crime scene. I try to pull into the underground garage, but I'm told it's closed due to a murder.

"Who was murdered?" I ask, concerned.

"Melora Stevenson," a cop says.

"What?!" I ask, in shock. Melora is my partner in *AmBITCHous*. We both invested in this magazine nearly a decade ago. Tears run down my cheeks. "What happened?"

"I'm afraid I cannot discuss this with you. For more information, you need to speak with Detective Carl Erikson."

I pull over to the side of the street and look for this detective. I have to find out what's happened; I'm beside myself with worry, beyond shocked.

Melora and I go way back to our freshman days at the university. I honestly can't believe she's dead. And on the morning she's supposed to make an important announcement, one that's going to affect all of our lives. She was going to announce our newest partner, who will also be one of the magazine owners. Melora had another surprise that not even I know about, but whatever it is, it was bigger than the new partner announcement.

I don't know much about this new partner other than it's someone from the outside and they're a former magazine owner. She just said it was someone of great influence who can turn our magazine business around for the better.

As I walk around the corner, my eyes catch a glimpse of a handsome man speaking with another attractive man, their appearances momentarily distracting me. For a second there, I managed to forget I was married with six kids. The oldest man looks up at me and signals for the other to stop talking.

"Excuse me, but do you know where I can find Detective Carl Erikson?" I ask as I approach them.

"Yes, I'm Detective Erikson, and this is my partner, Detective Julius Hunter. What can we help you with?"

"Hi, my name is Eva Santa Rosa, and I'm one of the owners of *AmBITCHous Magazine*. I was told that the founder, Melora Stevenson, was murdered? Can you please give me more information as to what exactly happened?" I ask.

"Well, from what we've seen so far, we gather it was a robbery gone wrong. It happened in the parking garage in her car. At first, we thought it was some kind of animal attack. From just the neck wounds alone, it looks as if her neck was torn wide open by some kind of giant claw. But the more we investigate, we're starting to think this was done by someone and maybe an animal got to her after she was murdered. The real cause of her death is unknown. We sent her body over to the coroner for an autopsy. Once we receive the reports, we'll know how she died and contact you with more information."

Just as he finishes, I look up to see Miyako walking toward us. She has no idea what's happened and she's business as usual. The other detective, Detective Julius, talks to her. From the look on her face, I can tell she, like me, is in pure shock and disbelief over the death of poor

Melora. I'm surprised she feels something for Melora, especially since Melora stole Miyako's ex from her years ago. Miyako never forgave her.

I amble back toward the garage and stand by Miyako's car, waiting for her. I already know she'll want to investigate this murder to see what really happened. Miyako has always been the "Sherlock Holmes" of our little tight-knit group. I often wonder why she never pursued a career in law enforcement or perhaps even a private eye. She would be damn good at those professions. She's always the one who loves watching crime documentaries—you know, the ones about serial killers, especially female serial killers, or the ones where women snap and kill their boyfriends.

She often says if things don't work out for her in the magazine world, she'll go back to school to pursue a career in law enforcement. That's where her heart truly is. I feel she became a partner just so she could be closer to Melora, maybe keep an eye on her. After fifteen minutes, I see Miyako walking toward me.

"Can you believe Melora is dead?" she asks.

"Honestly, as shocked as I am, yes. The bitch had many enemies, and most of them wanted her dead."

Miyako looks at me with raised brows. "What the...?"

"Yeah, I know. Trust and believe, if you knew what I knew, you would say the same."

"Damn! The fuck she ever do to you or anyone else for that matter?" Miyako asks.

"You really have no idea of what she's done?" It is quite possible Miyako may be in the true dark about any of this.

"I honestly have no clue what you're going on about. Has Melora done something to you?"

I laugh and stomp toward my car but pause and turn toward Miyako. "She's been fucking Roberto behind my back for over a year now."

Then I continue to my car.

CHAPTER 2

Miyako

I knew today was going to be fucked when I woke up this morning! My alarm didn't go off at 4 AM like usual, I missed my morning run, skipped breakfast, and ran late to work. On top of all that, Eva just dropped another bombshell on me!

"What the fuck? How do you know? Are you sure?" I ask in total disbelief.

I fire off one question after another, and I know it's probably irritating, but it's the detective in me. I also know Melora wasn't a saint and often did some shady-ass shit, like stealing one of my exes a few years back. I'm sure it wasn't the first time either, but I never would have thought she would do something like this to Eva.

"I'm absolutely sure. I'd rather not discuss any of that here or right now," she says.

"I totally understand. It's just hard for me to wrap my head around any of this. I know you wouldn't kill her, even knowing what she did, but who could want her dead? Not only do we have to worry about a possible killer, but we still need to run this company as if she's here with us."

She sighs. "Yeah, I know. We're in charge now."

~

Two hours pass by like the speed of light as we try and figure out what our next move will be. I tell Eva all about my conversion with the hot detective.

"As I was talking to Detective Hunter, I couldn't stop staring at him because of how fucking fine he is! I know now is not the time to be thinking about that, but I can't help it. That's not the only reason I want to get close to him. I want to stay up to speed on this investigation. This feeling is coming from me, like wanting to do something for Melora. We weren't as close as you two were, but I was trying. At the same time, I can't help but wonder... are we going to be safe from now on?"

"We have to leave the investigation up to the police. We can't get involved. Now as far as us being safe, we need to find out who this new partner was going to be and figure out what the hell Melora was up to that got her killed. It may have nothing to do with us or it could have everything to do with us. I also think we should hire security just as a safety precaution for us and our employees," Eva says.

"I doubt we're able to get into the office, let alone her private office, right now with the investigation still ongoing. Hell, we probably won't even be able to get into her home. This shit is fucked! Dammit, Melora. What have you gotten yourself into? Let's get together tomorrow and discuss what we'll do going forward. The company must still go on," I state.

"Okay, girl. We'll catch up with each other tomorrow. Maybe then I'll be ready to tell you more about Roberto and Melora's affair. We'll have to talk with the staff members and let them know what's going on and what our next move will be."

"Okay, honey. We definitely have to call a staff meeting as soon as the office re-opens. Try and get some rest. We will get to the bottom of everything. In the meantime, I'm going to speak with Detective Hunter again to see when we will be allowed back into the building to start making the necessary changes."

We hug each other for what feels like an eternity. It's exactly what I need at a time like this. I swear Eva has a magic touch because I instantly feel better.

I kiss her cheek as I say, "Drive safe and be careful. Text me when you make it home."

"You know I will, bitch. Love you!"

"Love you more."

I walk her back to her car just to make sure she makes it back safe and sound. I know I'll be safe here for a while because nothing has changed on the scene beside the fact the news crew has just shown up. I'm not getting anywhere near those cameras, so I turn in the opposite direction in search of Detective Hunter. It doesn't take me long to find him. He definitely stands out in a crowd.

He must be about 6'3", which I find incredibly sexy. I love when I have to look up to my man. What the hell am I saying? He isn't *my* man...yet. Let's not mention the way his arms and chest practically bulge out of his shirt, but not in a way that's too much or makes you think he's on steroids. No, you can tell he works hard to look that damn good. I'm a sucker for arms, and they give me all the feels right now. Sitting on top of his head is beautiful black hair, tapered on the sides, and has a slight flip to the end. His face is free of hair and looks smooth to the touch.

My favorite part of him has to be his cornflower blue eyes. My goodness, they remind me of the Antarctic Ocean with how beautifully blue they are. He. Is. Absolutely. Gorgeous.

"Hey, *l'amour*, are you okay? Do you need medical attention after today's events? Or do you require something... else?"

Did he just proposition me? I think he did or it could be a challenge. Either way, I'm game.

"No, I don't need medical attention. I just want to know who's responsible for the death of our partner. I know it goes against all protocols within the police world, but investigating is totally my thing. I said I would leave it to you guys, but I want to help. I don't mean to interfere with what you guys have going on, just me doing some investigative work of my own. You're welcome to join in on it, and other things, if you're down for it all."

"*L'amour*, you don't know what you're getting into. I'm not one of these boys that play around. If I want something, I get it. I've been eyeing you since you came on the scene, and I want to know more as well as give you and your friend some closure. So I'm down for whatever you want to give. I know what I want."

"Well, Detective, how would you like to have dinner with me? When the time is right, of course. We still have a magazine to run and a ton of employees to get sorted out, but I want to get to know you better."

"You've got yourself a date, *l'amour*."

"Why do you keep calling me that?"

"It's the nickname I decided to give to you. It's French."

"Aren't you going to tell me what it means?"

"Maybe over dinner I might. Who knows? Now, I have to get back to it, and I know you probably need some rest. Here's my card. Call or text me anytime you need me, especially regarding this case or even *anything outside of this case*. I leave the ball in your court."

I take his card as he walks me back to my car. He opens my door, and I slide in as I hear my phone ding.

It's a text from Eva saying:

I made it home, bitch. I'm going to take a nap before I have to tend to the kids!

I giggle because Eva is funny as shit and laughing is always good.

"What's so funny?" he asks.

"Eva; she's hilarious. It seems she has an affinity with emotions. I don't even think she knows that she does. At any rate, I welcome her and her gifts. They come in handy when I need them the most."

"Ah, Eva. That's her name. My partner, Detective Erikson, couldn't get out a complete sentence whenever her name popped up. It seems he was dazed when it came to her. We shall see what happens there, if anything. Get home safe and sound. If you need me, you have my number. Don't hesitate to use it."

"I won't. It was very nice to meet you, and I look forward to our date. Please, find out who did this. Have a good rest of your day," I say sweetly.

"You as well, *l'amour.*"

I make it home in about fifteen minutes and can't decide what I should do next. Dazed, stunned, and confused, I can't do much but worry. When I get like this, one thing that always helps is cleaning. I clean every nook and cranny from the moment I enter my house well into the wee hours of the night.

Too tired to do anything else, I take a quick shower and fall into bed. Moments later, I'm out cold.

CHAPTER 3

Eva

Twenty-Four Hours Later

I finally hear something from Detective Erikson.

I'm just finishing up cleaning the bathroom when I hear the doorbell ring. I check myself in our mirror wall to make sure all is well. I look like a mess as usual. Hair up in a messy bun, I'm wearing my favorite tank top and one of my husband's dirty sweatpants, and a pair of white socks. My eye makeup is a mess; I've been crying while scrubbing the toilet and wiping the tears away. House cleaning is always my go-to whenever I'm upset. Some cope with weed or alcohol, but I cope with house cleaning.

I do another quick check in the side mirror by the door. Everything is in its proper place. Detective Erikson looks as if he has been to hell and back, and honestly, I feel for the poor soul. He looks like he needs a little break or something.

His blue eyes have dark circles underneath them, almost as if he's not had any sleep in days. His dirty blonde short hair is disheveled and looks like he just got out of bed. That whole messy look looks good on him. I find myself getting wet in my nether regions. Shit, my clit is tingling and throbbing with pure ache.

The fuck is wrong with me? It's been so long since I've had someone that made my body betray me on all levels. Tonight, after the kids go to bed, I will have my wicked way with Roberto, whether he likes it or not.

"Detective Erikson," I say, smiling warmly at him before I continue, "please, come in! You look as if you could use a bit of a break."

I gesture toward him to come in. Good thing I cleaned house. Had this been a few hours ago, he would have thought there was another murder.

"Yes, I think it's best. I have some questions for you about the death of your business partner, Melora Stevenson," he says as he walks past me and waits for me to lead the way.

"Yes, of course. Anything I can do that will help you out, I'm more than happy to assist you with." I lead the way to the living room. Gesturing for him to take a seat, I ask, "Would you like something to drink or perhaps eat?"

"I would love some water, please. Thank you very much."

He's so formal and so professional. I have to admit, I find it very sexy. I can't help but notice Detective Erikson's scent; he smells like midsummer rain mixed with musk. Shit, I need to get out of here, I need to calm down. The succubus in me is beginning to wake up, and she wants playtime with the detective.

Entering the kitchen, I walk over to the sink and splash my face with cold water to calm my succubus. Inhaling deeply and releasing my breath slowly, I feel my hormones begin to calm down. Fuck, I was not prepared for that.

I grab a glass from the cabinet and rinse it out and then move to the fridge to fill it with ice cubes and dispense water over the ice. Once it's filled, I return to the living room where the detective waits for me. I hand him the glass of water and his hand lightly brushes against mine as he takes the glass from me. Again, he reawakens the succubus deep inside of me.

"Thank you." He smiles, and I turn to take a seat in the armchair not far from him. Trying my best to calm my succubus, I focus on him and what he has to say. "Did Melora Stevenson have a husband, boyfriend, or family for that matter?"

"No, she had no one. Miyako and I were her only family. She was seeing this new man, who she met online. We didn't know much about him other than that he was European, I think German, but not 100% sure. Why?"

"Her having no family makes sense as to why no one came to identify her body. We need either you or your partner to come in to officially identify her. I ask about a boyfriend or husband because in cases like this, they're always the prime suspect."

"Makes a lot of sense; they're closest to the victim. Miyako and I can come down to the police station later this evening. In fact, I can do so now," I offer.

"No, I think it is best if you have someone with you. It is not a pretty sight, and it may be very upsetting."

I agree. It will be best if Miyako comes with me. It wouldn't be fair to her if I do it alone without her; she needs closure as much as I do. Identifying her body will help.

"Yes, of course."

Deep in thought, memories of how I first met Melora back at the university come rushing back. We were both freshmen and roommates. My parents and I were setting up my side of the room and our bathroom when she came in with her parents. You could tell they were a power couple who looked as if they were in their mid-forties and professionally dressed. That must have been where she got her business mind and attitude from.

Miyako was our third roommate and the last to arrive. She came alone. Apparently; her parents were too busy to take her to college. So, she hitched a ride with a classmate who was attending the same school. An ex-boyfriend, so to speak.

God, how the three of us have changed over the years...

We're no longer the young college freshmen who met years ago. We're now powerful businesswomen who'd accomplished so much. Especially Melora. It was a shame she did not have a family, husband, or even a boyfriend to share her success and accomplishments with.

She had always been the one who put business and work first before her happiness and life. Her love life took a seat on the back burner. She always said, "Love cannot achieve true success or make you reach far in life. It is only a distraction from your true goal." Her goal was to succeed in life and make something of herself, someone she would be proud of at the end of the day. She also said love couldn't make you rich; if anything it attracted leeches, also known as broke, bum-ass men too lazy to work and make something of themselves.

Hearing the detective clear his throat, I look up to see he's watching me with those gorgeous sapphire eyes of his.

"Are you okay?" he asks.

"Yes, I am," I say, smiling at him.

"What time can you and Miyako come this evening?"

"Early evening. Miyako is coming by shortly. Once she arrives, we'll come in to identify Melora's body."

I can't help but wish the body they have isn't our fearless leader, Melora. Neither Miyako nor I have yet to see the body so how are we to know if it's really Melora? I secretly pray to God they have the wrong individual, that it's not Melora. My heart begins to break all over again as tears flood out of my eyes. My throat feels sore, and it hurts when I swallow. I hear the detective's cell phone beep.

"I have to go now, but when you arrive at the police station, please ask for either me or Detective Julius, and we'll come and get you," he says as he looks down at the phone and stuffs it back into his pocket. We stand, and I see him to the front door where he shakes my hand and hands me his card. "If you find out anything else regarding the death of your partner or if you remember anything else, please do not hesitate to call me."

"Yes, of course. If I come across anything, you will be the first to know."

CHAPTER 4

Miyako

Today is going to be a better day than yesterday. My alarm clock goes off at 5 AM on the dot. I press the stop button, pull the covers off me, and stretch my limbs. The first stretch is always the kickstart of my day, besides coffee of course.

I hop out of bed and make my way to the bathroom, where I throw on my yoga pants, tank top, and running shoes. Finished with that task, I make my way downstairs to the kitchen and grab a couple of sips of water before heading out for my run. I start my day off with a two mile-run from my house and back. This helps clear my mind and gets me prepared to take on each day. A much-needed stress relief.

I make it home an hour later, drenched in sweat but energized beyond belief. Once inside, I hightail it straight upstairs to take a nice, long, hot-as-Hades shower. As I let the water cascade down my body, I reflect on yesterday's events.

Melora being murdered, us taking extra safety precautions at work to ensure everyone's safety, Eva and I preparing to ensure *AmBITCHous* runs like normal, and me meeting Detective Julius... I know it seems like everything is moving so fast, but that's the thing about me—I'm going to live every day as if it's my last. You never know when it's your time to go.

This attraction I feel towards Julius is building as we speak. It's been a minute since I've had the pleasure of a man's touch, and since I can't have Julius just yet, I'll have to settle for the idea of him.

The hot water feels so good sliding down my wet body. I imagine the droplets are his hands. They caress every single part of me, and it is smooth to the touch. His big hands brush my hair to the side, exposing my neck to him for the taking. He peppers kisses along my neck, down to my collarbone, where he draws lazy circles until he reaches further down to my breasts.

His hands cup my size-D jugs as he begins kneading them in a delicious way that drives me wild. He lets his tongue come out to play with my hardened nipples. Ever so lightly, he licks and teases them until I'm a withering mess. At that time, he slightly nibbles on my left nipple and pulls it between his teeth, where he begins sucking on it. My goodness, I've died and gone to the land of mythical creatures. He then gives the same attention to my right nipple, and pretty soon, he has both my breasts pressed together so he can devour them at the same time.

I haven't even noticed when I slipped my hand in between my legs to caress my pussy into a mind-blowing orgasm. I rub my clit softly at first, but as my orgasm begins to take hold, the soft rubs turn rougher and rougher with the need for release. And release I do. It's not quiet or short, and it takes me a minute to come back down to earth.

"Whew, child, I needed that," I say.

There is a moment I feel ashamed for what I just did, but fuck it, you only live once, right?!

Satisfied for the moment, I grab a towel off the towel rack and wrap it around myself as I make my way to my walk-in closet. I begin toweling off while I walk around and pick out today's vintage wear. I always go for the '50s look with a touch of class. I slip into a green bow plaid blouse with a black skirt and pair it with my black Mary Jane high heel shoes.

I keep my makeup to a minimum with simple black eyeliner to bring out the green of my eyes. It's very rare for a woman of Japanese and Black descent to have green eyes, but I do. I paint red lipstick on my lips and blot it with a napkin, then apply a light layer of clear lip gloss to make it shine. My jet-black streaked with platinum blonde hair is pulled back into a low bun since I didn't take the care to roll it before I showered. I slip on my black watch and grab my green patent leather purse, and I'm ready to slay the day.

On my way out the door, I give Eva a call to see what's on our agenda today. "Good morning, Eva! How are you doing?"

"Aren't you just a little ray of sunshine this morning? What the hell has gotten you all hyped up? How many cups of coffee have you had?" she asks.

I giggle. "Today is going to be a good day. I feel it in my soul. Things went accordingly, like they do almost ninety-nine percent of my mornings, and I feel we may get some good news about what happened to Melora. I'm ready for whatever comes my way today."

"Well, ain't that something? Are you sure it has nothing to do with Detective Julius's fine ass?" she questions.

"I mean, not him per se, but the thought of him..."

She laughs. "Girl, stop talking in riddles. Did your nasty ass have a wet dream about him?"

"You know what, trick, I'm not discussing this over the phone with you. I really called to see how you were feeling and to see what we have on our agenda for today, but here you are, with your nasty ass all up in my business," I say as I roll my eyes as if she can see me.

"I'll let that slide for now, but you have some explaining to do! As far as what we have going on today, I'll fill you in once we make it to the office. One of the most important things we have to do is view Melora's body. We should handle that first just to get it over with. I don't think I can wait till evening to do it."

"Yeah, I'm not looking forward to that at all. By the way, have you ever met Detective Erikson's sexy self? I don't understand how we got paired with two hot as fuck men such as them. I always encounter men old enough to be my grandfather trying to get a piece of my pie." I laugh.

"Hell yes! He came by this morning, and I swear my inner hoe wanted to come out and play. I don't know what got into me, but I can tell you that he wanted me!"

She howls with laughter. She's laughing so hard at her joke that I join in. It lightens the mood with all we have going on today.

"Bitch, you're fucking crazy, and I love it." I laugh. "You should let your inner hoe come out to play. I know I plan on letting my wild side come out when the time is right, of course. We have to think straight and be on our p's and q's in order to catch a killer. Look at me, sounding like I'm a real detective on the case."

"First things first, we need to take care of our people at the office. I suggested we amp up security, and I mean it. Next, we have to view Melora's body, and then I say we get together and make a list of those who we know Melora fucked over. I was her closest friend, so I know ninety-five percent of them. You, on the other hand, can use your skills to figure out who the other five percent are. Once we get that list together, hopefully things start to get clearer," she states matter-of-factly.

"There is still the underlying question of who she was bringing on to become the next partner of the magazine and why. That's going to answer some questions I have lingering in my head. I'll be sure to write those down, too. I don't want to forget or leave anything out," I say.

"Okay, girl, let's get this day started!"

"I agree, let's get this day started!" I shout as I put my hand up for a high-five, forgetting that we're on the phone and not face to face. "Oh, dammit!"

"You had your hand up for a high-five, didn't you?" she asks. She knows me too damn well.

"Yep, I sure did. Look, I sometimes forget, okay?!" I laugh.

"Girl, you are so crazy, I'll see you in a few," she says as she hangs up.

CHAPTER 5

Eva

As I stare down at Melora's lifeless body on the slab, memories of when we first met come flooding into my head again. Even at such a young age, Melora was fierce and beautiful.

I remember watching her in awe and admiration as she entered the room as if she owned it. My parents paid her no mind but to someone like me, at that age, she was magnificent. I heard my mother calling my name in the distance, but I was so taken by Melora that I didn't hear her. The next thing I saw was my mother standing in front of me with a very angry look, pulling me out of it and back to reality.

"Where the hell were you?! Didn't you hear me calling you for the past five minutes?!" my mother snapped.

I rolled my eyes. My mother always had a flair for dramatics. "I was taking a breather, forgive me," I said, watching Melora as she got settled.

My father stepped in to put me in my rightful place. "Watch how you talk to your mother."

"I'm sorry, Mother."

Melora watched the entire thing go down, unaffected by any of it, carrying on with her business of getting settled. Miyako soon arrived, and I was glad to see her. She was the only one who reached out to me during the summer as a way for us to get to know one another better before we met. Miyako was quite a character, who I instantly loved and adored. Miyako was the crazy one of us three, the most adventurous and outgoing. She would say she was the boldest, but I think Melora was probably the boldest of us three.

"Are you all right over there?" I hear Miyako ask.

Snapping out of my brief flashback, I look at Miyako. She's staring at me with concern. I wipe a tear from my eye.

"Yeah, I'm good. Just reminiscing on when we first met back in university."

Miyako looks like she's taking a trip down memory lane, too, and she laughs. "Who would have thought we would be this close? Like blood sisters?" she asks. "Even back then, that heffa always managed to get whoever and whatever she wanted, especially our men. Do you remember the fights we had whenever she fucked any of our men?"

"Yeah, I do. She nearly destroyed me and Roberto before we even started," I answer, but I'm not laughing because it was one of the darkest moments in my life.

"Bitch, you nearly killed her when you two fought! The RA had to intervene and almost removed you from the room. Lucky you and Melora kissed and made up. But seriously, even back then you were protective with Roberto. I can't blame you. You and he always had something good. Melora envied that. She envied you the most, to be honest," Miyako says as we leave the morgue.

"I know she did. Which is funny, as I always had the utmost respect for her and admired her most."

Detective Carl Erikson calls out to me. I turn to him and smile. I feel my heart skip a beat and a flutter of butterflies explodes within my stomach. This is silly! I feel like a high school girl gushing over the hot football quarterback. I really have no business feeling this way when I'm happily married, but the succubus in me is anxious...and who am I to deny her the pleasures of this very attractive detective who's eyeing me as if he's about to take me right here?

"Yes, Detective?"

"Do you mind staying back for a few moments? I need to talk to you about a few things."

"Yeah, sure! I can do that!" I say, sounding a little too enthusiastic.

Trying my best to tone down my excitement, I look at Miyako and ask, "Do you mind going ahead without me, hun?"

Miyako stares at me with those dark, knowing eyes of hers, as if she knows what I'm up to. "Of course, we can talk more tomorrow at the office." She smiles wickedly and winks at me.

Shaking my head, I feel my cheeks heat up. Detective Erikson watches me with those gorgeous eyes of his, filled with something that makes me crave him all the more. My clit twitches just a little from just how he looks at me alone.

"Please come with me to my office, where we can have more privacy."

He turns and heads down the hall as I follow close behind. Once I enter the office, he closes the door and grabs my hand, pulling me closer to him.

His gorgeous eyes fill with such dark, intense hunger. My clit throbs deeply. He looks at me as I lick my lips, and then he pulls me in to kiss me softly, flicking my tongue ever so slowly and teasing me a bit. Purring into the kiss, I let him taste me as I kiss him back. He tastes so good that I squirt just a tiny bit.

He moans as he deeps the kiss, claiming my mouth in such a heated, passionate kiss. My large breasts press into his strong muscular chest, making me all the wetter. He's devouring my neck, tearing my blouse open. I feel his tongue licking my neck hungrily, and I throw my head back, aching for more than what he's already giving.

His breath is hot on the swells of my voluptuous breasts, and the thin lace bra that holds them in is next to go. He growls as he rips my bra off with his teeth alone, exposing my breasts to him. His tongue wraps itself around my large, erect nipples, and he bites into them softly, tugging at them and making them taut.

My clit throbs with soreness as he continues to tease me. Warm, sweet milk squirts out as he tugs on my nipples and his tongue hungrily laps up the milk. I close my eyes and moan, enjoying every second of this.

"I fucking want you here and now," he growls softly into my ear.

"Oh, fuck! I have wanted you since the second we met," I purr back.

"Make love to me," he says, looking me in the eyes.

"I can't..."

"Why not?"

"I'm married."

"I don't care! I want you! I must have you!" he demands.

Pulling away from him, I say, "I can't!" as I get myself together and walk out of the office.

I'm not exactly sure what just happened, but whatever it was, it can't happen again.

I'm a married woman with six kids. I must set a good example for my girls. Even though I'm a succubus, I need to set a good example of how a woman is supposed to act. I have to practice what I preach, but part of me aches for the detective. Part of me regrets walking away from him just now. But another part of me is proud for doing the right thing.

Yet... his touch lingers on my body, reminding me of what could have been, setting me on fire. He awakened something primal deep inside of me, something which only he and he alone can satisfy.

CHAPTER 6

Miyako

After I leave Eva with Detective Erikson, I decide I need to chill and relax. Seeing that it really was Melora's lifeless body on that cold table has me thinking; life is just too short to not live in the moment. Sure, I want to go home, fill up on Ben and Jerry's while watching Netflix and cry my eyes out for the loss of Melora, but I can't. I can't dwell on the horrible sight of seeing her like that. I will miss her fiercely, but I have to continue. So, I decide to give Detective Hunter a call. I just need to talk to someone.

He picks up on the third ring. "Detective Hunter, talk to me."

"Hello Detective, it's Miyako Lee. We met the other day at *AmBITCHous Magazine.*"

"Oh yes, how can I forget? How are you doing today?"

I sigh. "I'm doing okay. Just needed to talk to someone."

"Is everything okay, Miyako?"

"Yes and no. Eva and I viewed Melora's body, and I wasn't prepared, I suppose. I mean, yes, people I know have died and I've seen dead bodies before. and Melora and I weren't *that* close, but it just hit different if that makes any sense."

"It makes sense. Death has a way of making us feel different things with each person, whether you're close to them or not. Death wants to be heard. It is up to us to give it what it wants or let it consume us. I've seen so much death in my time as a detective that we're old friends. I can't let it win, and that's why I try and solve each murder—to give death what it wants. There isn't a case yet that I haven't solved," he says.

"That's pretty impressive. Do you have a secret talent that no one else knows about that helps you solve *every* murder?" I question.

"Now, that's for me to know and you to find out... if you can," he challenges me.

"You haven't known me long enough to understand that when someone challenges me, I accept. I don't back down, ever, and I detect a challenge in your statement. So trust *me* when I say, challenge accepted. You've been warned."

"I love a woman that goes for the gusto. We never did have our date, and I think now is a good time to cash in on it. What do you say, *l'amour?*"

"I'd love some company. Eva is probably going to be tied up for a while. What the hell, let's do it. What did you have in mind?" I ask.

"Well, I'm not sure how comfortable you are with coming to my place, but I can cook one of my Cajun cuisines for you, pair it with a movie and store-bought ice cream; or we can go out to dinner, a movie, and ice cream. The choice is yours."

"Hmm, both options sound very enticing. I don't think I want to be around others at the moment, so I choose to come to your place where you will wine and dine me, put on an amazing movie or two, and we'll pig out on some delectable store-bought ice cream," I say happily.

"Good choice. I will drop you my location, that way you can find it easier. Once you get here, we'll take a trip to the store to pick up all the ingredients for dinner and ice cream. While I make dinner, you can pick out a movie for us to watch."

"Okay, Detective, it's a date. I'll see you soon," I say.

"Please, call me Julius. Detective sounds so formal or like we should only use the title when we mean business," he says, laughing.

"Okay, Julius, see you soon," I say as I disconnect the call.

It's funny how just talking to someone can calm your nerves. Whether they say the right thing or what you need to hear, there is always some sort of comfort within their words. I'm looking forward to spending some time with him. I haven't enjoyed a man's company in a while and it's past time that I should.

Pulling up to my home, I contemplate what movie we should watch. I get out of my car and make it to my door when I notice it is slightly open. I know damn well I closed and locked the door when I left. The detective in me wants to barge in and demand who may be hiding in the shadows to come out, but the rational part of me says to call Julius. So, that's what I do.

"Detective Hunter, talk to me."

"Julius, it's me again...it looks like someone may have broken into my home."

"Where are you right now?" he asks.

"I walked back to my car and called you. I didn't want to go in alone in case someone is still inside."

"Good thinking, I'm on my way. Sit tight, lock your doors and stay on the phone with me."

"Okay. Just for the record, I really wanted to go inside and demand answers."

"Trust me, I know. You seem like a detective in training, but you did the right thing by not going in and calling me first."

"I know, and thank you for saying that. Once we find out what happened here tonight, I'm still going to your place. Later, I'll give Eva a call and explain what happened and see if I can crash at her place until I change the locks and have an alarm system installed."

"I know we just met, but I have two spare bedrooms at my house and you're more than welcome to take one while you get things situated," he offers.

"Oh, no. I couldn't do that. I don't want to get in your way."

He chuckles. "Trust me, it's quite alright. You won't be in the way. If anything, you may liven up the place."

"I'll think about it. Thank you so much for the offer."

"Anytime. You can hang up now, I'm here," he says as he taps lightly on my window.

"Should we go in together or are you gonna make me wait outside?"

"I prefer you wait, but I know you won't, so follow my lead. I'll go in first, give you the all-clear, and then you may enter."

"Sounds easy enough; lead the way."

He kicks the door open and steps inside. He switches on a light and doesn't see anything, so he pops his head out the door and says, "All clear. Come in and let's take a look around."

When I walk in, I turn my head from left to right, looking around the kitchen and living room. I notice nothing seems to be out of place. No visible damage that I can see. We venture up the stairs, Julius first and me hot on his heels. There are two rooms up here, my bed/bathroom and my office. We check the office, and all is clear. He goes into my bedroom first. I follow in right behind him.

"Nothing seems to be missing," I say.

"Okay, that leaves the bathroom. I'll go check it out," he says.

I walk around the room and head into the bathroom. I notice he's staring at the mirror. What I see has the blood draining from my face.

Written in red lipstick are the words:

"YOU'RE NEXT."

Everything goes black.

CHAPTER 7

Eva

I feel his soft lips on mine as his tongue slowly flicks my own. Gazing deep into his gorgeous eyes, I am now under his mysterious spell. His fingernails dig deep into my flesh as he pulls me closer to him, and his massive, thick, hard cock deep inside of my tiny, tight, wet pussy has me wanting more and more. He rubs his thumb over my throbbing nipples, making them harder, and I moan as he moves down to my neck. The feel of his hot breath, his teeth biting and nibbling on my flesh makes me cry out his name.

Soon, I feel him near my ear. In a deep, rough voice, he whispers, "I want to devour you right now," which only makes me want him all the more.

Breathing heavily, I pull away to look into his eyes. Eyes so dark and intense they're almost scary; such intense hunger that makes me wetter. Biting my lower lip, I pull him closer to me and feverishly kiss him. I call out his name.

"Eva?" Roberto calls out to me in the distance. "Eva!"

Again, I hear Roberto calling out to me, and this time, someone shakes my body. My youngest, Gracie, is crying for me.

Slowly, I open my eyes...

. . .

Roberto is looking at me, his eyes squinted.

Shit, I hope I wasn't talking in my sleep again, I think to myself.

Thank God Roberto is an Incubus and understands such dreams. He has them often.

Climbing out of bed, I take Gracie from her father and carry her down to the kitchen to get her some breakfast. She's not feeling well and very cranky.

"Hush, my sweetness, Momma's getting you some breakfast," I soothe her as I check her temperature. She's still warm. "I think we need to take her to the doctor. With this new virus going around, we can't be too careful, especially with our children. I'll schedule an appointment later on this morning to get her checked out," I say to Roberto and hand her over to him.

"See if you can get something as soon as possible. It's been twenty-four hours and she still has a fever."

"Yes, of course. I need to go into the office today, so you need to take her since you're off."

"Are you sure that's the best thing to do right now? With a killer on the loose?" he asks, concerned.

"Well, the business must go on. We can't let this killer run our lives. Also, Miyako will be staying with us for a short while. Someone broke into her house, and she needs a place to stay for a day or two till she changes her locks and installs an alarm system."

"Shall I fix up the usual room for her?" Roberto asks.

"No, you can put her in Mom's room for the time being. It's only a day or two."

"Baby, what was your dream about?" he finally asks.

I stop what I'm doing, turn toward Roberto and say, "Oh, it was nothing. It was just a sex dream."

"Who is Carl?" Roberto asks, looking at me suspiciously.

I already know what's going through his mind. "It's no one."

"Are you cheating on me again?" he asks.

Roberto doesn't hold back this time and he doesn't care if the kids are around. His eyes turn darker and more intense, signs of his anger starting to show.

"Of course not! Are you crazy?! You know you and the kids mean the world to me and are my everything!" I walk over to Roberto, kissing him deeply and passionately. "Baby, I am so blessed to have you as my soulmate. I will never do anything to mess up what we have, I promise!"

He's unresponsive to my kiss. Something's up, I feel it. But this isn't the time or the place to discuss it.

"We need to talk this evening when you get home from work after the kids have gone to bed," Roberto says.

"Talk about what? Is everything okay?"

"No, everything is not okay," he says angrily.

Gracie bursts out crying, and it's a hunger cry. She's also in pain. I feel for her. But I can't be late. I look at Roberto who says, "Don't worry, I got this. Go to work."

He tends to poor little Gracie. Her face is red and she's screaming in pain and hunger. My heart breaks hearing her little painful cries, her balled fists clenched so tightly that her knuckles are whitened.

Dear Lord, whatever is going on with my baby girl, I hope it is nothing serious.

A tear rolls down my cheek as I get in my car and drive off to work. When I arrive, Detective Erikson is waiting for me in my office with his partner, Detective Hunter, and Miyako.

"Ladies, we have a lead on Melora Stevenson's killer," Detective Erikson announces, looking at Detective Hunter.

"Do either of you know Kip Shiloh?" Detective Hunter asks.

"Yes, he is a photographer we hired a few months ago to do a high fashion shoot for us during fashion week in Milan."

"Why?" Miyako asks, sitting in one of the seats.

"Are you aware that Melora Stevenson was having a secret affair with Kip Shiloh?" Detective Erikson asks.

I raise an eyebrow in shock. "No, I had no idea. Melora was happily married to a wealthy banker. I had no idea she was cheating on her husband. I wonder how long this has been going on."

"The autopsy showed that she was about twenty weeks pregnant," Detective Hunter says.

Both Miyako and I are shocked by this bit of news.

"We have reason to believe Kip Shiloh is the father," Detective Erikson says, looking at Miyako.

"Do you think he is the killer?" I ask.

"We cannot say, as it is still an open investigation. But we have a few leads that we're following up on to learn more about this case," Detective Hunter said.

"Well, that is all we have for now but there is something else you both need to know," Detective Hunter says before asking, "Did you know Melora was about to file for bankruptcy and was in the process of selling *AmBITCHous*? From what we learned, it looked like the magazine was in deep debt and you're on the verge of losing it."

This is the first time Miyako and I are hearing about this. We look at each other in shock and disbelief.

"How can this be?" Miyako asks, still in shock.

CHAPTER 8

Miyako

We've not only been hit with one bombshell but *three* all in the span of five minutes, and I'm still trying to process it all. I'm not sure how Melora could have let the magazine go into so much debt that she would need to file bankruptcy. Then she was pregnant and cheating on her husband with the newly hired photographer.

"What the actual *fuck*, Melora?" I ask no one in particular. "Eva, how do we fix this? We can't let the magazine go down. We are still a part of it with or without Melora. Tell me how to fix this?" I say.

"I'm angry, hurt, mad, and sad. It bothers me that all this was going on right under our noses and Melora hid it from us both. No offense, Miyako, but Melora and I were closer. I would think she would have told me sooner before things got so serious. I guess no matter how close you are to someone, you never really know what's really going on until it is too late," Eva says.

"That's *it!* I've had it up to *here* with all this *bullshit* that's fucking going on. First, Melora is murdered, then my life is threatened, *now this*?! All her secrets are coming out for us to deal with. This is too fucking much! I'm gonna blow up at any given time if I don't start getting some damn answers!" I yell.

It is Detective Hunter that speaks up first. "I know how you feel, but we'll get to the bottom of this to find out why all of this is happening or has happened. First, you ladies need to be careful from here on out. Second, Detective Erikson and I will do everything in our power to find out who murdered Melora and broke into your house. Third, get the ball rolling with the locks and security system at your place. Most importantly, stay calm and continue with things. That's about the best advice I can offer you ladies at the moment. We will be here if and when you need us."

"Thank you, Detective. I feel a little more confident that everything will be okay," I say.

"Okay, let's get a plan in place. Miyako will have the security company install a new security system in her place. In the meantime, she'll stay with me. Next, we will find out more about our new photographer and what he has to say about all this," Eva says.

"We'll contact both Melora's husband and Kip Shiloh regarding this case. From here on out, please leave the detective work to us, the professionals. We can't have you ladies interfering with an open investigation. And please be careful; just act normal around Kip Shiloh. Do *not* share any of this with him or anyone for that matter. Everything is confidential," Julius states.

"We will keep it professional. Eva, do you have the number to Freedman's Security Company?" I ask.

"Yes, let me get it for you." She rummages through her purse for their business card. After what feels like an eternity, she finally finds it and hands it to me. I take out my cell and give them a ring.

"Hello there, this is Miyako Lee. I'd like to schedule an appointment to have my locks replaced and a security system installed at my home. Can you send someone out today?" I pause for a bit as they check their schedule, and when they come back on the phone with an open time slot, I reply with "One hour is perfect. Thank you so much and I'll meet the technician there." I rattle off my address to the receptionist.

"Okay, ladies. In the meantime, be careful. Call us if you need anything or any help," Detective Hunter says.

I notice Detective Erikson has been quiet since announcing all the news about Melora. I also haven't missed the sly glances he's been sending Eva's way. While I think she doesn't notice, something in me tells me she does but won't act or acknowledge it.

Eva seems to be in another world, so I lightly tap her on the arm and ask, "Are you ready to go? We have an hour to kill before we meet with the technician at my house. I don't want to stick around and grab any of my things so maybe we can do a little shopping to get me some essentials before we head back to your place."

"Yeah, shopping always makes you feel better. Let's go," she says.

We wave goodbye to the detectives and head to our cars. Once there, we make our way to Target to pick up a few things.

CHAPTER 9

Julius

"I notice you've taken a liking to the girl. Don't let her mess with your head. We have to be careful around them. Not because I don't trust them; it's because I don't want your secret to be exposed. We could use your special talent in this case," Carl says.

"I know what I'm doing. You don't need to worry about me. Eva is who you should be worrying about. Those looks and glances you kept sending her way didn't go unnoticed by any of us. Care to share what's going on there?" I question.

"No, I don't. Let's make it back to Miyako's house before they arrive so you can use your sixth sense to catch a whiff of who broke in. We don't need the girls finding us, so let's be quick about it," Carl demands.

We leave in a hurry and make it to Miyako's place in record time. Once we pull up, I get into the back seat and look around to make sure nobody can see what I'm about to do. I'm a shapeshifter, which allows me to change into any animal I need to get the job done. This time, I shift into a black wolf. Their tracking skills will come in handy at a time like this.

Carl opens the back door for me, and I leap out. Making my way to the front door, I catch the faint scent of another paranormal being and a human.

"Are you picking up on anything?" Carl asks.

I give a small howl that means yes. I push open the door with my nose and wander around downstairs. I'm picking up the same scents from outside the door all around here. Turning, I head upstairs. Once there, I head into Miyako's office, then her bedroom. Here I pick up Miyako's scent, which reminds me of gingerbread cookies, and it smells so delicious.

But I'm also picking up something else...It smells like rotten meat. I begin scratching the floorboards and whining as Carl comes into the room and asks, "Have you found something?"

I howl as he pulls a knife from his back pocket and begins prying up the board as I continue to scratch. We're so engrossed in trying to get to whatever is underneath here that neither one of us hears rustling until it's too late.

"Why are you in my house? Is that a fucking wolf in my bedroom?" Miyako screams.

Carl and I look at each other and I have no choice but to do what I think is best. I fall and play dead. After all, I'm not trying to frighten the ladies. That seems like an understatement because my wolf form is three times bigger than my human form, making me look beastly and intimidating.

Carl speaks up. "Of course he's not a wolf. He's the special task force unit's dog that we sometimes bring in to further assist us with our investigations."

"If that's true, why is he so big and playing dead right now? I see you peeking, buddy. You piss or shit on my floor, and I'll kill you. Never mind that. Where is Julius? You guys are almost always together," Miyako asks.

"He stayed behind at the precinct. He should be along shortly," Carl says.

"I'll just give him a call. I want him to be here when the tech from Freedman's shows up," Miyako says as she goes to dial my number.

Before Carl can make up another lie, I decide to shift back into human form. This draws a gasp from Eva, who has been silent since arriving, and a scream erupts from Miyako before she faints. I once again catch her before she hits the floor and wonder how the hell I'm going to explain this.

CHAPTER 10

Miyako

I'm not sure why I fainted. I've met a lot of paranormal beings in my life. I guess maybe he just caught me off guard, and with all the stress of everything else going on, I just couldn't handle it. It seems like they're in a compromising position because for one, why are they at my home without notifying me, and two, what the hell could they have found?

Julius caught me before I hit the ground, which is good because I'm only out for a split second, and when I come to, I'm ready for war. "Um, care to explain what the *fuck* is going on here? Carl? Julius? Someone better start talking before I flip out even more than I already am!" I scream.

Julius decides to speak first. "Miyako, I can explain. Follow me into the kitchen please."

I follow close behind him because I don't want to miss a thing and the view he gives me is really something.

"Okay, I'm here, start talking. Better yet, put something on. I can't talk to you while you're naked." I grab a towel I don't remember putting on the countertop.

He grabs the towel and begins. "First off, I'm a shifter. I have special abilities that help me solve every case I work on."

"Okay, so why all the secrecy? I understand we don't know each other well, but every time we take one step closer to getting there, something happens and we take two steps back."

"I know, babe. I was going to tell you once we had our date, but something always comes up. I'll try harder because I don't want to mess this up before it even has the chance to take off." He pulls me in for a tight hug.

I can already feel the anger leaving me. I pull back slightly and go to place a kiss on his cheek, but he turns his head at that moment and captures my lips in a mouth-searing kiss. I moan into him as he takes his fill of me. Too soon, it ends and I'm a little dizzy from the spell of that kiss.

"When you kiss me like that, it makes all my troubles go away. For the time being, that is. But seriously, you're going to have to tell me more about you being a shifter and what powers you have. It all sounds interesting and dare I say cool. I wish I had powers, but I'm nothing special," I say.

"Yes, babe, I'll tell you all about it because we are definitely going on that date. I have many things to share with you and not just about myself, but also about this case."

"Great, it's settled. We're having our date tonight. After this hellish day we've all had, I'm looking forward to relaxing."

CHAPTER 11

Eva

As I listen to Miyako, my mind drifts off to Detective Erikson. My inner succubus craves him like a junkie craving her drug of choice. There's something about him that draws me to him. I shouldn't feel nor think this way for another man who is not my husband, but I can't help it. As I said, there's something about him that draws me to him like a moth to a flame. I suddenly find myself yearning for his touch, the feel of his lips upon my own. My pussy gets moist from just thinking about his sensual kisses. The way his tongue makes my clit twitch and tingle for so much more.

Turning to Miyako, I excuse myself. I make up some excuse, anything that gets me out of the house so that I can go to him.

"What the fuck is wrong with you, bitch?" she asks.

"I just remembered; I have to pick up a prescription."

Looking at her cell phone and then up at me with a raised eyebrow, she replies, "Bitch, you're lying. What are you up to?"

Fuck, this bitch knows me better than anyone else. Nothing gets past her. I shift uncomfortably under her suspicious gaze.

"Bitch, you're itching for that hot-ass detective, aren't you?"

I blush softly.

"I fucking knew it!" She bursts out laughing. "My little chickadee has a secret of her own! Well, shit! Don't let me hold you back, girl! Go handle your business with Mr. Detective Erikson!"

"Please keep this to yourself. It's not me. It's my succubus side, which has this little itch," I say.

Miyako knows of my inner succubus and promises to keep it secret. She also knows my husband is an Incubus, who, like me, from time to time has sex with others, which is okay with me as long as at the end of every night, he comes home to me. That's what matters.

"Detective Erikson?" I say into my phone the second I close my car door.

"Eva? What's wrong?" he replies

"I need to see you immediately."

"Yes, of course. What's this about?" he asks with concern.

"I just need to see you right now!" I say with urgency in my voice.

"Okay, I will text you my address."

A few moments later after ending the call, I receive his text with his home address. Blissfully, no one's out on the roads. Any cops must be preoccupied with something else.

I speed through the city to Detective Erikson's house. Although it's a forty-five-minute drive, it feels like fifteen. Pulling up in front of his house, I sit in my car for a moment, contemplating whether I should go forward. Ever since meeting him, I've had this strong desire for him. The circumstances of Melora's death don't matter to my succubus. She always gets what and who she wants no matter what's going on.

I take a deep breath and exhale slowly and open my door. His front door opens, and he stands in the doorway, waiting for me. He's shirtless with just a pair of jeans on and bare feet. Sweet Lucifer, help me tonight. Normally, I'm not like this. I'm hesitant when it comes to sex and getting the deed done, but there's something about this man that has me feeling very vulnerable. When I reach him, he invites me into his home. I walk in slowly, looking around.

"Thank you for seeing me on such short notice."

"Yeah, sure; no problem. What's wrong?"

"Nothing really, other than the fact that ever since we met, I cannot stop thinking about you," I say, fumbling with my keys nervously.

"Really?" he asks softly.

"Yes, I feel as if I am back in high school, nervous around the hottest guy there." I laugh, staring at the ground to avoid eye contact, fearing that I will lose all self-control when I look into his gorgeous eyes.

He laughs, a laugh filled with warmth and sincerity. Oh, how the sound of his laughter puts me at ease, just feeling the warmth spread around me like fire. Daring to look up and into his eyes, I see nothing but genuine appreciation. I also sense something else, something stronger and more intense. He's holding back as well.

"You know, I have to admit, I've felt the same as well. But since you're a married woman..."

I swallow hard. "Why didn't you say anything?"

"It would be unprofessional of me, especially under the circumstances in how we met. It was like fighting a losing battle, holding back from just taking you right then and there. To fight that strong urge to kiss you deeply and passionately every time I see you. You've already rejected me once." His eyes fill with hunger and desire.

Pulling me close to him, he takes me in his arms and looks deep into my eyes. For a moment, it seems as if his eyes change colors, and I feel an explosion of butterflies deep within my core. Before I know it, his lips take mine in a hot feverish kiss. His tongue pries open my lips to claim me with just a kiss alone.

He deepens the kiss, and as he does, he growls deeply, making my clit twitch with desire. I feel something sharp brush against my lower lip. Pulling away slowly, I look at him. As if he read my mind, he gives me that knee-weakening, sexy smile of his, which reveals something I never expected. Protruding from his mouth is a pair of sharp fangs. His eyes take on another almost fluorescent color.

I gasp in shock and cover my mouth, blinking in disbelief. I know I have no business being surprised since I am a succubus. Supernaturals are such a rarity that I sometimes forget they co-exist amongst mortals and other Supes like my husband and me. I reach out to touch his fangs, as if touching them will make some kind of difference.

"You're a vampire?" I ask.

"Yes, I am. How could you not know? The moment we met, I immediately picked up on the fact that you're another supernatural, a succubus."

"I should have but for some reason, I did not."

"I know I should have said something sooner, but I wasn't sure if I could completely trust you with such a secret." He pulls me in closer for another hot passionate kiss.

"It's okay. I sensed there was something about you, but I never could put my finger on it. I just felt this strong connection with you," I say, kissing him back and breathing deeply.

Pulling away from me, he slowly undresses me, kissing my soft, exposed flesh along the way. I purr, enjoying the feel of his warm lips on my flesh. I feel the sharp tip of his enormous fangs gently caress my flesh. My heart skips a beat from that feeling alone, anticipating what's to come next.

He reaches my thong and pushes the thin piece of lace to the side to lightly flick my swollen, throbbing clit. I moan and feel my knees begin to go weak. I throw my head back and my eyes roll upward. He continues to lick and tease my delicate womanhood, making me wetter and wetter.

I grab hold of his soft, silky hair and clutch a handful, moaning softly as he continues to tease me. I feel the tip of his tongue lightly run along the opening of my pussy.

"Sweet Lucifer…"

I'm unable to say anymore. Gently, he slides one finger, then two, in my dripping pussy and proceeds to thrust deeply but slowly as he sucks on my clit. The feel of his mouth on my hypersensitive tip makes me throb deeper to the point where it hurts.

"Mmmm, fuck!" I say under my breath.

The familiar sensation of an orgasm building up to the point of explosion deep in my core takes over. I fight back the urge to cum so soon with every fiber of my being, but it is getting so hard. Breathing heavily, I feel my heart pounding ever so powerfully within my chest as if it is about to explode at any moment.

Pulling away from me, he stands and unbuckles his pants to release his massive, hard cock. My eyes widen in disbelief; it is so huge and thick. My mouth waters at the sight but before I have time to admire such a beauty, I feel him lift me against the wall, and I wrap my legs around his waist. Staring deep into his gorgeous eyes, I feel the tip gently brush up against my wet opening. The tip alone makes me even sorer.

Biting my lower lip to hold back a whimper, he enters me. He takes his sweet time, and my tight pussy stretches to accommodate him. I fight the urge to squirt all over his cock before he is deep inside of me.

Once he is fully inside of me, he begins to thrust deep, slow, and gently. Making sure I am comfortable and not in any kind of pain, he watches me. With warmth in his eyes, we take our time making love until we feel the need to go faster, harder, and rougher. We sync up, together we are one, moving in rhythm and motion together. Our hearts pound powerfully. His grip grows tighter, and the feel of his nails digging deep into my flesh only makes me want him all the more.

Unable to hold back anymore, he explodes within my womb like an erupting volcano that's shot its lava deep from within. In a matter of moments, I feel myself cumming again. We continue as if we are one, making sweet, passionate love, looking into each other's eyes, and getting lost in the moment as if time has stood still. Reaching another climax, we cum together, over and over, until we can't cum anymore. He carries me to his bedroom and lays me gently on his bed. He climbs in, pulls me close to him, and holds me tightly. Resting my head on his chest, I feel the powerful vibration of his heart. I close my eyes as his heart lulls me to sleep.

A few hours later, I wake up to look at the time I see it is almost four am.

Fuck! What have I just done? I think to myself.

Quietly, I crawl out of his arms and out of his bed, trying my very best not to wake him. Making my way to his living room where we made love only hours ago, I collect my clothes and head toward his front door, getting dressed along the way. Like a thief in the night, I speed away.

CHAPTER 12

Miyako

I know Eva is going to partake in some extracurricular activities, which has me thinking...

Since she and Detective Erikson will both be occupied, that'll give me time alone with Julius. Of course, there's still the matter of me finding out what they were doing and what they may have found out, not to mention, I'm still a target and I have no clue who the culprit is.

I notice a van pulling up that looks suspicious, but once it gets closer, I see the Freedman's Security Company logo plastered on the side. I breathe a sigh of relief I didn't know I was holding and turn to Julius.

"Will you stay with me while he takes care of the alarm system and installs the new locks I purchased?"

"Yes, I will. I find myself wanting to do anything for you, especially when it involves your safety. I don't know what it is, but as long as I get to have you to myself, I'm all in."

"You can't say things like that to me! I'm a hopeless romantic and will read more into that than you know," I say, blushing.

"Aww, you're so cute when you blush. I wonder what else makes you blush that shade of pinkish-red," he says as he walks closer to me.

I take a step back and say, "Hold it right there, Mister! Don't think you're getting off that easily. You still haven't told me why you guys were here to begin with and if you found anything. Did something tip you off? If so, I would like to know what it is," I say aggressively.

"You're even cuter when you're mad and try to put your foot down like you could actually take me. I'll let you in on what we found, but only after they finish setting everything up. I don't want others to know what we're discussing." Sniffing the air he says, "He's a Supe, by the way."

"Well, duh. I'm not oblivious to the underworld. Why do you think I called this particular company? Not only are they Supernaturals but they are the best. Plus, I trust them more than I trust most humans."

He shoots me a knowing look because I just hit him with the word *duh*. He seems stunned and that has me laughing my little ass completely off. I'm laughing so hard, I snort.

After a few minutes, he begins to laugh as well before saying, "You think you're so funny, with your words and that little snort-laugh. Just wait until I have you alone. You'll be doing more of that blushing from before."

I know that look and it's going to end with us tangled in the sheets... together.

"Words don't mean shit to me. I trust in action. Action always speaks louder than words alone and backs up words in more ways than one. Show me, don't just tell me," I say as I push a wild strand of hair behind my ear. I don't want him to know that I'm affected by his words.

"That can be arranged. We are having our date at my place tonight. I know you're supposed to go over to Eva's house for a day or so but cancel that. Because tonight, you're *mine*." He growls.

If that isn't one of the sexiest things I've heard in a long time, well then, I don't know what else it could be.

"Oooh-kay then. Let me go and check to see how much longer the security guy will be and then we can go from there," I say as I quickly slip away, not giving him a chance to touch me or say anything. I needed some time to cool off because I'm about ready to pounce and have my way with him. Not that that's entirely a bad thing, I need sex to live. It's a rule, right?!

"Thank you, Shawn, for coming out so soon to get me set up. I appreciate it," I tell the technician.

He looks at me with lust-filled creepy eyes, staring at me from head to toe. Of course, when he comes back to my boobs, he's practically salivating at the mouth as he says, "Anything for a pretty, sweet thang such as yourself."

I'm not even sure what happened next, but I see a ball of fur fly clean across the room and land right smack dab into Mr. Sleazeball's chest.

"If you don't put your fucking beady ass dog eyes back into your big head and stop eye-fucking what's mine, I'll rip your got damn throat out!" Julius growls.

"How would I know she was yours? She doesn't have your scent on her. My apologies. Now would you kindly get the fuck off me so I can leave?" Shawn shouts.

"She doesn't need to have my scent on her to earn your respect, although it will be there sooner rather than later! You're on a fucking job, and that is *not* how you act. Would you like it if I reported you to your employer? No, right? Then start acting like you have some fucking common sense and not as if you're a pup learning about women for the first time!" Julius shouts as he lets go of him.

"Ma'am, I am so sorry. I'm not sure why I'm acting like this, it's very out of the ordinary for me and I apologize. Please accept my apology and I will forever be in your debt," Shawn says.

I must say, he looks apologetic, and he is just a kid, so I'll let him slide this time and take him up on his offer. Never know; he may grow up and come in handy when danger may strike. Danger... who the fuck says that?

"Okay, Shawn. You have yourself a deal. Please find out what has you all frazzled up and nip that shit in the bud. Don't want you trying this with someone else who may not be as understanding as we are," I tell him.

"Not at all, ma'am. Anyways, you're all set. Here are your keys, security code you can change using these instructions, and here is the invoice. The alarm needs to be set when you leave, and once you come in, you have ten seconds to disarm it before the police are notified. Right here is a panic button if there is ever an intruder and you can't leave the house. It's silent but will notify the police. If you have any further questions, this is my card. It also has the company info on there should you need it. Thank you for your time, patience, and understanding. You all have a great day," he says as he gathers his things and leaves.

I turn to Julius and say, "Jealous much? Stop eye-fucking what's *yours*? Your scent isn't on me *yet*? Care to explain all of that, Mr. Grouchy-pants?" I question him. I honestly can't wait to hear what he has to say.

He stalks over to me, grabs me around the waist as he says, "Sure, *l'amour*, I would love to explain what I meant. But first, go pack and call Eva to let her know you're staying with me tonight."

I'm so caught up in the moment that I wrap my arms around his neck and deepen the kiss. He tries to pick me up, but I push out of his grasp because there is no way I want to do anything here just yet.

"Hold on there, tiger, if we keep this up, we're gonna end up fucking on the floor and I don't want that... yet," I say.

"Then hurry up and pack so we can go back to my place."

He sure is bossy, but I like it. The strong dominant type: yes, he will do nicely. I don't even answer him, I just turn around and make my way to my room and throw some things in a bag and call Eva. It goes straight to voicemail.

"Hey, Eva, just calling to let you know that I'll be staying with Julius tonight. Call me tomorrow, love you, bitch."

I skip down the stairs a moment later. "All packed," I say as I lean in to place a peck to his cheek heading for the door. He heads out first so I can set the alarm and lock up.

We make it to his truck, and he helps me settle in. He heads to the other side and slides in behind the wheel and the next thing I know, we're off. Not giving him any time to change the subject, I start my investigation.

"So, tell me, why were you and Detective Erikson at my house tonight?"

"When I was there with you earlier, I picked up the scent of another Supernatural being. I'm almost positive it was a vampire, but I wasn't too sure. So, we came back so I could shift and find out more. I was on my way to dig something up, but that's when you came in and derailed what I was about to do. I smelled something underneath the floor in your room," he tells me.

"What?! Turn around, we have to go back and see what it was you sniffed out!" I shout.

"No, we aren't turning back. Detective Erikson and I will go back tomorrow and investigate while you ladies are at work. We all still have jobs to do. Trust me when I say we will find out what it is. Plus, Shawn was right. My scent isn't on you and therefore every male human and Supernatural will try and get with you. *L'amour,* you are mine, and I am about to claim you with my scent. You're getting marked tonight."

He growls the last part, and I'm instantly turned on by that.

"Marked as in, fucked or like *marked*?" I question.

"Both. I don't know what it is about you, but I don't want anyone else to have you. I want you all to myself, so I hope you're ready for a night you will never forget," he tells me.

"Hell yes, I'm ready! I can tell you're one of the good guys, but if you screw me over, I'll put a spell on you," I tell him while twitching one eye for good measure.

"A spell? Are you sure you're not a witch? Only witches talk of casting spells on people." He laughs.

I sigh. "Pretty sure I'm not a witch. I'm just a boring ole human being."

He grabs my hand and says, "Nothing is boring about you, but you never know, you could be a witch or a siren because I am definitely under your spell."

"Wow, you're so romantic," I say, rolling my eyes.

We pull up to his driveway where he hops out and opens my door for me and grabs my bag while leading the way to his home. It's beautiful, a full-on bachelor pad, but it works for him and his career.

Once we're inside his home, he drops the keys in the holder and my bags on the floor. He has a predatory look in his eyes, and I'm his prey. I take a step back as he takes two towards me. I'm backed into a wall with nowhere to go because I wouldn't know where to run anyways. I'm in his territory.

"Are you scared, *l'amour*?" he asks as his eyes change from brown to black.

"Um, should I be? Maybe I am. Maybe I'm rambling. I'm a nervous wreck because I'm not sure what I should do—"

I don't get to finish what I'm saying because he has me caught up in another mouthwatering kiss.

This time when he goes to pick me up, I let him. I slip my arms around his neck and my legs around his waist, and it feels like I was meant to be here. I feel his hardness press into my throbbing wet-ass pussy, and it's *huge*.

He breaks the kiss, but only to begin worshipping my neck. He alternates between peppering kisses along the base with nips of his teeth. Before he makes his way back to my lips he says, "Now *l'amour*, this won't be sweet and slow. It's going to be hard and fast. We have all night to go sweet and slow but if I don't have you now, I'm gonna explode."

"Well, what are you waiting for? Less talking, more action!" I say to him breathlessly.

While I unbuckle his pants, he slides his hand down my body and does the same to me. I shimmy out of my pants as he picks me back up. I begin to wrap my legs around his waist as he says, "Brace yourself, *l'amour*, this might hurt a little."

He slams into me, and it is pure heaven.

I scream as he enters me because he is, in fact, bigger and thicker than any other man that I've been with. He presses his lips to mine to take my mind off him filling me up because he isn't even in all the way. It hurts but at the same time feels so fucking good. Am I weird to like this or is this normal for a guy his size? I don't care either way.

He keeps pushing in, and I swear, it gets better and better. Once he's in all the way, he breaks the kiss with a pop of our lips, looks at me, and smiles as he starts pounding my pussy into oblivion.

"Oh. My. Goodness. Julius!" I shout.

"You okay, *l'amour*?" he asks.

"I am now, don't stop!"

"As you wish," he says as he fucks me relentlessly against the wall.

His hands are all over me. He uses one to turn my neck to the side to give him better access where he starts with kisses, then his hand is around my neck, and I swear I see stars. I love it. Choke me, Daddy, but not to the point of death. He's picking up the pace now, and I can feel my orgasm building.

"*L'amour*, are you going to come for me?" he asks seductively.

"If you keep fucking me like this with your hand around my neck I will," I confess.

"Then let go, because the minute you come is when I will mark and claim you as mine."

"Do it!" I shout.

He thrusts into me and that pushes me over the edge. I see stars, I'm falling. This is the fastest yet best I have ever come in my life.

He takes this time to bite my neck. I yelp in pain, but that soon turns to pleasure because he is still pounding into my pussy. I feel another orgasm building and it seems stronger than the last. He bites again. I scream and cum all over his enormous dick as he howls and shoots his hot seed deep into my sore pussy. The sight of him is literally the hottest thing I have *ever* seen.

His eyes are black; he has some of my blood on his lips and sweat coating his forehead. But that's not the best part. His razor-sharp teeth are still extended, and they are shining like diamonds right now.

"Wow! That was fucking *hot*! How I have been missing this is beyond me," I tell him.

My legs are still wrapped around his waist as he leads us to his bedroom. He lays me on the bed and goes to the bathroom to get a towel. He comes back and begins cleaning me off, then himself. He throws the towel on the floor and lies in bed beside me.

"Are you okay? I didn't hurt you too badly, did I?"

"I'm a big girl, and I can handle most pain. But no, you didn't hurt me. In fact, I loved every minute of it. We definitely have to do that again," I say, yawning.

"Oh, this isn't over, but we do need to rest first. Let's get some sleep and see what happens when we wake up."

"That sounds like a plan," I say as I lean over to kiss him.

After that, I turn my back toward him where he pulls me closer and wraps his arms around me. We drift off to sleep in no time. What dreams may come while I sleep?

CHAPTER 13

Eva

The next morning, Miyako and I meet up for brunch. She's staying with Detective Julius Hunter and from what I hear, things are starting to spice up between them. I never was one for gossip, but I swear Miyako has the juiciest gossip on this side of the Mississippi and I can't wait to hear the details of her first night with Julius. I pull up in front of the little corner bistro named Little Slice of Heaven, where Miyako and I normally meet to catch up on the latest gossip.

I see Miyako is already at our usual table, waiting for me with a silly grin on her face that says she got some dick last night. Raising an eyebrow, I set my handbag on the floor by my chair. She's glowing, and I can't help but smile at her and laugh.

"Well, damn! He must have really rocked your world!" I say.

I sit and take a sip of my water, waiting for her response. She blushes deeply. Now, this is so unlike the freaky Miyako I know who has no filter nor have I ever seen her blush.

"Let's just say, he *more* than rocked my world." She sips her tea, looking around to make sure no one is in earshot.

"Oh? Is that so? Do spill the tea, girlfriend."

Ironically, the waitress has just brought me a cup of warm tea.

"Well, after the security company installed the new system and locks at my house, he took me back to his house where things got a little heated. I suspected he had a thing for me, but I never knew..." she pauses for a moment, looking around again, "I just never knew the extent of it."

I nearly choke on my tea and blink in disbelief. "Come again?"

"Girl, the first time we made love, it was so fast and hard, my pussy is still sore as fuck. But you should have seen the size of his cock. It's so huge and thick that I think he might have torn my pussy because right after the first time, I bled a little."

"Damn!"

"The way he made love to me, especially the first time, was sooooo fucking good. I've never felt this way. I suppose that's because I was only with boys before and Julius is one hundred percent man! I think it is safe to say, he is the one."

She smiles so brightly it warms my heart to see her so happy.

"Aww, Miyako! I'm so happy for you! You deserve nothing but the best of the best and all the true happiness this world can truly offer you!"

I get up from my seat and hug her tightly. Miyako has come a long way since our college days when she was messed over and over by thirsty-ass fuckboys who used and abused women. Frat boys; such a disgrace to the male gender.

"Girl, I think my days as a single woman are now officially over because shit, I think he claimed both me and my pussy last night!"

We both burst out laughing. I haven't laughed this hard in such a long time. But shit, it's true. Detective Julius Hunter has tamed the "freak" in my girl, and she is now officially his woman.

"Oh, my God! I totally forgot about you and Detective Erikson! What happened? Did you get some dick from him?!" Miyako asks, pulling away and sitting back in her seat.

Now it's my turn to blush deeply as I sit in my seat across from her. Taking a sip of my second cup of hot Chai Tea, I glance around as if it's some kind of top secret. Miyako watches me intensely.

"Girl! Quit playing around and spill the fucking beans! Did you get some Detective Erikson dick or not?!" she whispers.

"Yes, I got some and then some," I say quietly.

She raises an eyebrow. "What does *'and some'* mean?"

"Looks like you weren't the only one who got claimed last night."

"SAY WHAT?!" she exclaims, her eyes widening in disbelief. "But you're married?!"

"So? A married woman can have a secret lover. Even if she is a succubus," I say with a secretive smile.

"Oooh, girl, you're playing with fire now!" Miyako says.

She knows all too well it's forbidden for a succubus to get this close to her lover, especially when married to an Incubus. I know I have to tell Roberto about Carl at some point before it's too late. I just don't know when.

"Are you in love with Detective Erikson?" Miyako asks, concerned.

"Yes. That's the crazy part. A Succubus can have multiple lovers including a husband if she chooses. But it's always been known that Succubus can only love one and he has to be an Incubus. Now what I am about to tell you, you must take to your grave as there's more to Detective Erikson than meets the eye."

I know I can trust her with what I'm about to tell her, but she's also not supposed to know this little fact.

"Yes! You know I can keep your dirty little secrets! What is it?!"

"Well, Detective Erikson is a Supe like me."

"Wait, what?" she asks, confused. "You mean he is an Incubus like Roberto?"

"No, love, he is a vampire," I say.

"Get the fuck out of here! You mean to tell me there are vampires, too?!"

"Huh? What do you mean?"

"Shit..." She looks down at her lap like she's said something she shouldn't have.

"Miyako, what are you not telling me?" I ask. Now I know she's keeping something from me.

"Detective Erikson and you are not the only Supes on the team, girlfriend."

"What do you mean?"

"Julius is a shifter."

"Get the fuck out of here! Seriously?!" I ask incredulously.

"Yes, but promise me you won't tell another soul. You're not supposed to know. And from what I saw, Detective Erikson is well aware of this fact," she confesses.

"I swear I won't tell a soul. I'll play stupid," I say.

"I always sensed something Supernatural about him. We can usually sense each other," I state.

Miyako looks at me thoughtfully. "Really? Now *that* I did not know."

"Yeah, I pick up on a Supe from miles away. But of late, I haven't been picking up Supe vibes since they are a rarity. Unless you're in New Orleans; that place is nothing but Supes."

My phone begins vibrating next to me. I grab it and tap the green phone icon to answer it. "Eva Santa Rosa, how can I help you?"

"Eva, this is Carl. There has been another brutal murder. I need you to come down to the police station as soon as possible. It is someone close to you."

My heart drops as I hear myself ask the question to whose answer I dread. "Who is it?"

"It's your husband, Roberto."

Tears well in my eyes. I look up at Miyako, who's listening in on the entire conversation and already knows something is up. "I will be down there in the next fifteen minutes," I say as I put the phone down. "Miyako, I need you to take me to the police station right now."

Miyako doesn't ask any questions. She grabs her stuff and leaves money on the table to pay for our brunch. We rush out to her car, and within the next fifteen minutes, we're at the station.

CHAPTER 14

Miyako

Eva is frantic and hysterical as we walk through the doors of the police station. She's just been informed that Roberto has been brutally murdered. I can't even begin to imagine what she could be going through. This is *not* something she—or we, for that matter—need. We're still trying to process the murder of Melora, a potential suspect, the break-in to my home, and now this. This will break her. I know she loved Roberto with every fiber of her being. Of course, they had their ups and downs, but there was nothing they couldn't overcome.

We make it to the front desk and just as Eva is about to start asking questions, Detective Erikson comes from around the corner and pulls Eva into a tight embrace.

"I'm so sorry. I don't know what else to say to make it better besides we will find out who did this."

"I know you will. I just can't believe this. I won't accept this. He can't be dead. We just saw each other this morning before I left for brunch with Miyako. He was on his way to work. How would someone find the time to murder him in between? I just don't understand any of this!" Eva screams.

"Eva, baby, calm down. You're gonna make yourself sick. This isn't the time or place to lose it. You still have your babies to think about. None of this makes sense, but I know the detectives will find who did this. Please, let me help you," I tell her as I pull her into a bear hug.

"Miyako, why does all this bad shit keep happening to us? What have we done wrong? *Who* have we done wrong? My babies, how am I going to tell them that their father is dead? Oh God, what am I going to do?" Eva begins sobbing.

At this point, I don't know what to do. I think she needs to be sedated, but don't want to do that to her because she still has to be strong for her kids. Not to mention, she still has to identify his body. That's going to be the hardest part.

I look at Detective Erikson and ask, "What can you tell us about what happened?"

"His throat was slashed, and he was stabbed multiple times. It wasn't a quick and easy death as one would hope, but after his throat was slashed, it didn't take long for him to perish," Detective Erikson states.

Eva begins howling now and it is my undoing. I can't stand to see her hurt like this. I walk her over to a bench and tell her, "Eva, honey, I'm going to make a call. Can you sit right here and wait for me?"

"Where else am I going to go? My heart is somewhere in here, lying dead on a table, waiting to be identified. Yes, I'll stay here," she says in a robotic state.

I pull out my phone and make a call to someone nobody else knows about. She is my herbal and spiritual mother. A few years back, I was going through it with one of many fuckboys, and she found me. She helped me through some tough times. She is a witch, but one of the good ones. I know she'll be able to give Eva something that will help her during this traumatic time.

I talk quietly into the phone. "Auntie Em, it's me. I need your help."

"What is it, chile?" she asks me.

"It's my best friend, Eva. Her husband was just found murdered and a few days ago our partner, Melora, was also murdered. She's in dire need of some relaxation, but she also still has her kids to worry about. Is there anything you can do or make that will help her through this?"

"Chile, now you know if you would just embrace this side of you,

you could do this yourself," she tells me, and I have no idea what she means.

"Auntie, you always speak to me in riddles I've yet to figure out. Do you think you can cut me some slack and just tell me?"

"No, baby. Unfortunately, it doesn't work like that. When the time is right, which will be sooner rather than later, it will all make sense to you. Now, you and your friend come over to see Auntie and make haste," she tells me as she ends the call.

Leave it to Auntie to keep me in the dark. She's not my real aunt, that I know of, but she is the closest thing to one and I know I can count on her when needed.

"Eva, honey, there's somewhere I need to go, and I need you to come with me. Can you come with me, sweetie?" I ask her. I know I'm speaking to her like a child, but I don't want to upset her and I'm trying to keep her calm.

"Detective Erikson, is it okay if before Eva goes in to identify his body I take her somewhere really quick?" I ask Carl.

"I suppose that won't be a problem. The sooner you're back, the better, though, so please keep that in mind. We need to catch the killer. We aren't sure it is the same killer, but we are doing everything possible to find out. Go now."

"Alrighty, Eva, let's go."

I hold my hand out to her. She eyes it suspiciously before she looks up and sees it's me. Slowly but surely, she places her hand in mine and together we walk out of the police station.

"Where are we going?" Eva asks me.

"We are going to see Auntie Em. She has something for us, or rather you," I tell her, hoping she'll go along with it.

"Okay, Miyako, I trust you. I'm just going to close my eyes for a bit. Wake me when we are there."

"You know I will," I lie to her. I'm going to let her sleep until I figure out what Auntie has to help her.

We're there in less than ten minutes. Eva is still out cold and that works in my favor. I walk up to Auntie's door, and it magically opens before I can knock. It's not weird that that happens, I just need to know how she does it.

"In here, chile. Why did you leave your friend outside?" she asks. Now how can she see all that? It must be a witch thing. "You would be able to see it, too, chile, if you just open your eyes and give in to yourself."

"Auntie, how in the hell can you hear what I'm thinking? And there you go, talking in freaking riddles again. I mean, why can't you just come out and tell me what you mean?" I ask her, getting more and more frustrated.

"Chile, it isn't up to me. I can only tell you so much. Now go and get your friend so I can give her a little something that will help her."

I turn and make my way back to the car to grab Eva. Shaking her awake, I say, "Wakey wakey, Eva. We made it to Auntie's house, and it's time to go in. Let me help you."

"I really wanna scold you for treating me like a kid, but at the same time, I know why you're doing it. I just want you to know I appreciate you so much and I'm grateful to have you as my friend." She pulls me into a hug and begins to sob.

"It's okay, honey, I got you. Let's get inside. Auntie is waiting for us," I tell her as I walk us inside and we make our way to the kitchen, where Auntie is stirring something on the stove.

"Come on in, girls, Auntie is just about done. Miyako, baby, I made you a little something too," she tells us.

We take our seats at her round kitchen table as she places two cups of steaming hot tea in front of us. It looks and smells like a simple chamomile with lavender tea, but knowing Auntie, that's not the case.

"What is it?" I ask, eyeing the cup of hot liquid suspiciously.

"No questions asked, just drink. It will make you both feel so much better. Trust Auntie, she knows what you need and when. This has been a very trying time for both of you ladies and I want nothing more than to help in any way I can. This will help you figure out all the riddles and hints I've been dropping."

"Oh, no. That shits not creepy at all, Auntie, but I love and trust you. Eva, you ready to drink our pain away?"

"Yeah, girl, let's do this!" She sniffles as we both take deep pulls of the tea Auntie has provided for us.

"Drink it all in one gulp now, girls. It's better that way," she tells us, and we oblige.

"So, how will we know it worked?" I ask.

"Oh, trust me, you will know. Now, don't you girls have some business down at the station to attend?"

Dammit, how does she always *know*?

"Yes, Auntie, we do. Thank you so much for coming to our aid. I do hope this helps Eva and allows me to decipher those cryptic messages you've been sending my way. We'll go ahead and make our way back down to the station. Detective Erikson is waiting on us."

"No worries, chile. He is patiently waiting for y'all. Now go ahead. When you have questions, I can provide you with guidance and some answers. Don't keep me waiting."

"Oooh-kay, Eva girl, are you ready to go?" I ask as I get up from the table.

"Yeah, babe, I'm ready to goooooo," she slurs.

I'm not going to question Auntie's antics, but I'll keep a close eye on Eva to make sure she's all right.

We make our way to the car and in a matter of minutes; we're back at the station. I don't feel any different and begin to think maybe Auntie was pulling my chain with all her mambo jumbo back there. As we get out of the car and make our way into the station, I'm hit with a wave of nausea.

Eva sees my step falter and rushes over to me. "Damn, bitch; did Auntie slip you some jungle juice into your tea?" She giggles.

I can't even be mad at her; she giggled. That's a sure sign her concoction is working its magic. As for mine, I have no idea what's going on. We make it up to the desk, and just as we're about to ask for Detective Erikson and Hunter, they both come to our rescue.

"Miyako, baby, what's wrong?" Julius asks me.

"I don't feel so well. I went to see my aunt because I wanted her to make Eva something that would help her, but she made something for me, too. Now, I feel like I just need to sleep, but I can't. I have to be here for Eva and the kids."

It's Eva who speaks up first. "Miyako, sweetie, if you're not feeling well, you don't have to stay. I have Detective Erikson with me, and I'll meet the kids later. Plus, I'm feeling pretty good right now. I mean, don't get me wrong, I am still mad as fuck and torn as shit that this happened to Roberto, but I need you at one hundred percent. We are in this together, and if you're not all there, we'll both be no good. Now get your ass home, or to Detective Julius's place, and rest."

"How the hell did the tables turn? I'm supposed to be taking care of you! No, I can't leave you."

At that moment, I double over in pain. I nearly hit the ground, but Julius is there, picking me up before I can make contact.

"Get her ass out of here now! She's hard-headed and won't listen to me. You have to take her and go," I hear Eva tell Julius.

"You don't have to tell me twice, Eva. Carl, I will be in touch soon. Keep me posted if you find out anything or you need me. For now, I'm going to try and figure out what's wrong with my girl," Julius tells them.

"Auntie, she said all would be revealed in due time once I drank that tea. I have a feeling that time is now. Take me home, Julius," I tell him as the world goes black.

"Don't worry baby, I got you," Julius says. As he drives us home, I fall in and out of sleep. Dreaming, I must be dreaming.

"Or remembering," I hear Auntie say.

CHAPTER 15

Miyako

Miyako Dreams Her Memories...

AGE 2

"You're not completely human... you're special but too young to know about any of this. We have to erase it from your memory. If we don't, it will only make matters worse. I wish it didn't have to be this way, daughter, but you're too powerful for your own good. If the other covens find you, they will make you pay for our sins. To keep you hidden, we must erase any memories of your old life. One day, when the time is right, we will be reunited. We love you forever and always."

AGE 5

"Frank, she's getting stronger. She shouldn't be able to do any of this being that she's a level-one witch. She's doing things that take even a level-seven witch years to master. Her mother said this would happen and told us who to call. I just hope this doesn't hurt her in the long run."

"Judy, we were given specific orders when we took the child in. We were not to ask questions. We were to raise her as humanly as possible and call this number should she show any signs of her powers getting stronger. Now the time has come for them to work their magic again and keep our baby girl safe. No questions, just actions."

"I know, I just hate this. How will we explain this to her when her memories come back? How will she ever trust us? I don't know how much longer I can do this, Frank. I love her too much! I know she isn't our biological daughter, but dammit, she's *my* child."

"Judy, it's for her own good. Nobody is taking her away from you as long as we keep this whole charade up. Now stop worrying and grab my phone. I have the number on speed dial."

"Hello, dear. It's time I presume?"

"Yes, Auntie Em, it's time."

AGE 13

"You freak! How did you do that?"

The class bully wants to know how I threw a rock at her without even blinking an eye. Heck, I wanna know, too. That's not the only thing I've been able to do.

I hear other people's thoughts, move things with my mind, and I've been able to talk to animals. It's all weird to me, and I have no idea where it's coming from. I mean, I could tell I was different, but I had no idea any of this was even possible.

Talking to animals just popped up out of the blue. I normally talk to myself because I don't have any friends, there's this lonely little squirrel that looks like she needs a friend, too. Before I know it, I'm pouring my horrible day out to her, and right when I'm about to get up and leave, she speaks back to me and tells me everything is going to be okay. She also says she's a great listener if I want to talk more. I'm scared shitless and excited at the same time.

I can't wait to tell my mom. After I confess everything to her and Dad, they both look at each other with weird expressions and say, "We have to call her again. Her memories are coming back."

They must have forgotten I could hear them because Dad flips his phone out and calls someone while Mom goes into the bathroom. She comes back out with her hands behind her back. Of course, they're talking without using words, just using their eyes. I see Mom pass something to Dad as he switches the phone to the other ear and comes behind me.

I feel the faintest prick on my neck and hear Dad say, "We are sorry, sweetheart, we will take care of everything."

Then the world goes black.

AGE 17

I'm so angry I cry. It begins to rain outside. I stomp my foot several times on my bedroom floor and hear thunderclaps outside. I feel so much rage, I step to the window in time to see a lightning storm happening. I walk past my dresser mirror and do a double-take. Looking back at me is a girl with white stormy gray eyes.

I get a closer look at myself and see a storm brewing within my very eyes. What the hell is going on?

I run to the window, look outside, and then make myself cry. Magically, it begins raining. I stomp my feet time and time again and hear the raging thunderstorm that happens with each hit. I summon up all the anger I'm holding at my parents for grounding me over standing up for myself and see the sky turn black and lightning bolts begin to rain down.

How is this even possible? There is no way I'm doing any of this.

Mom comes rushing in out of breath and says, "Baby, what have you done? They will find you. You have to calm down. Frank! Quickly, go lie down and close your eyes, silently cry as if you're having a nightmare. I hate we have to keep doing this, but you're too strong for your own good. One day, baby, all will reveal itself. Close your eyes now. Your father is coming."

"What is it, Judy?"

"It's time again. Look, she's crying in her sleep and causing the storm outside. You must call Auntie again."

"Calm down, Judy. I'm on it. Baby girl will be okay. Everything will be okay."

AGE 21

"Oh, excuse me, chile, are you all right?" an elderly lady stops and asks me as she sees me crying on the sidewalk.

"Yes, ma'am, I'm fine. Boy problems," I tell her as a way of explanation.

"I remember those days and don't miss them at all. Tell me, chile, does it always rain when you cry?"

"Hmm, what a weird question, but to tell you the truth, ma'am, it usually does. Maybe I'm just bad luck or something because I seem to cry a lot lately and it always rains," I confess.

"You're not weird or bad luck, chile, you're unique. I've only known four other people whom this has happened to. How long has it been going on?" she asks.

"I'm not sure. For as long as I can remember, which is beginning to become a challenge. I feel as if there are blank spaces in my life, but when I think I've got it all figured out, it's all gone again. It's unexplainable."

I have no filter when it comes to this lady. Maybe she's just easy to talk to, I think.

"Or maybe it's because I'm a witch with special abilities," she says.

"There are no such things as witches nor are there things that go bump in the night. Now, if you will excuse me, I have other things to worry about," I tell her as I stand and get ready to leave.

"Chile, you have much to learn, but unfortunately, now is not the time. When you're ready to learn about the Supernatural world, you come and find ole Auntie. She knows best, but don't wait too long. Those blocks that have been put in place won't last forever." She turns and walks away.

"How will I find you should I decide to come back?" I yell.

She turns and blows me a kiss and says, "You will know, chile."

I'm hit with a sudden wave of familiarity. I know when I'm ready to find out what those riddles she was spewing are all about, I just have to jump in my car, and I will be guided to her.

AGE 27

More and more things have been happening that I can't explain. I decide it's time for me to pay Auntie a visit. The only thing is, I don't know where she lives. I walk to my car and hop in. I turn on the radio and pull out of the drive, not sure where I'm going. I figure I'll just drive around for a few until I get a hunch on where to go next.

Turns out I don't have to wait long. Fifteen minutes later, I pull up to an older house out in the sticks. There are no other houses around, and it's hidden well behind all those beautiful trees. I don't remember making it here, but I do remember Auntie telling me that when I was ready to find out more, I would be guided to her.

As I get out of my car and head up the stairs, the front door opens before I can knock. "Come on in, chile," I hear Auntie call. "I've been waiting all day for you. I'm so glad you're finally here."

"How did you know it was me?" I ask.

"Baby, I told you when you were ready to know about the supernatural world, I would be here waiting for you, so that's what I was doing. Waiting. I knew you would come. So, first things first, I'm a witch, and you are, too. I'm not supposed to tell you just yet, but since I will have to take away that memory, for now, I want you to know. The things that go bump in the night are real and so is the Supernatural world. Vampires, werewolves, fairies; all of it. Now we don't have much time. The only thing I can let you be fully aware of is the Supernatural beings of the world. You won't remember that you're a witch until the time is fully right. Quickly now, ask any questions you have about me and the paranormal world."

"You're a witch? Vampires, werewolves, fairies are all real? That's not possible, is it?" I ask in disbelief.

"Yes, it's possible. Deep down, you already knew, but when your memories began to resurface, they had to be blocked again. The timing was never right," Auntie tells me.

"When will the time be right?" I ask, trying to make sense of it all.

"Not for a few more years, when darkness strikes. I will be here to help you throughout the waiting period, but for now, I have to put the block back in place. Don't worry, chile, soon."

Sleep claims me.

PRESENT

I wake up in a pool of sweat and yell, "I'm a witch!"
Auntie, I have to go see Auntie, but first, I need Eva.
"Julius! I need Eva, quick!"

CHAPTER 16

Eva

It's been two weeks since the murder of my beloved Roberto, and we've laid him to rest. All our family and friends came together to celebrate his life, including Detective Carl Erikson. This man truly is a saint. He's been there for me throughout this entire ordeal. He even stayed with me to help me with the kids.

Miyako also stops by daily to check in on me and the kids to make sure we're okay. She helps out with the kids as well and cooks for us. Both she and Detective Hunter, along with Detective Erikson, were there with me during the funeral arrangements, which was the hardest part of this entire thing. Every time I thought about burying Roberto, I broke down in tears and was unable to think clearly. My entire world felt as if I'd died along with him. If not for my children, I would have wanted to die with him. Anything to be with him again, I would have done.

Detective Erikson holds me close to him at night, watching over me as I sleep. He began sleeping in my bed when I started having horrible dreams that made me cry out in pain and devastation. I have nightmares of my dead husband and his lifeless body. The police are nowhere near finding who the killer is, but they suspect it is the same individual responsible for Melora's murder.

After the funeral, I ask my mother to take the kids for a couple of weeks while I heal and recover. She's more than happy to take them off of my hands and even suggests keeping them for a couple of months. I agree to her keeping them for the summer. My mother is my guardian angel. Being a succubus herself, she understands Detective Erikson is just what I need during these dark times.

"Thank you for everything. I don't know what I would do without you," I say, smiling at my mother warmly.

"Believe me, I more than understand what you're going through. You forget, your father was murdered when you were a young child and I, too, went through the same thing that you're going through right now." She hugs me tightly and rubs my back to comfort me. "Let Detective Erikson take good care of you, love. He is just what you need to heal from this. Trust me. Your succubus side will need to feed soon, and he is just the one. He is not your typical man, and he can handle the venomous kiss of a succubus."

"What do you mean?" I ask, confused. My mother always has a way of knowing things that no one knows about.

"He is a vampire, my darling child," she says, caressing my face.

"Yes, I know. He told me he was a vampire. That's why I am so drawn to him, even when Roberto was alive."

Detective Erikson enters my room and says, "The kids are sound asleep."

My mother looks at him and smiles. "Thank you so much for being here for Eva and my grandchildren. You are an angel for being so dedicated and devoted to a woman in need during such dark times."

"It's nothing. I only want what's best for Eva and her children. I'm just looking out for them, as it is second nature for me to be so protective of those for which I care."

"I can see that. You have a beautiful soul with so much love and protection to give. I know I have no business even thinking this, but honestly, you are so good for my daughter. I'm glad she has you in her life."

"She is very special and deserves the best," Detective Erikson says, looking at me with such warmth and love in his gorgeous eyes. I can't help but blush.

~

THE NEXT MORNING, after my mother leaves with the kids, Detective Erikson turns toward me and asks, "Why don't you let me take you away for a week to my mountain cabin?"

He strokes my hair, watching me with those beautiful eyes of his.

I could use a getaway from all this chaos and madness. From the memories of Roberto. I need a moment to heal from his death. "It would be nice to get away for a week. Yes, I think that's a good idea," I say to him and then kiss him softly.

He holds me tightly, pulling me closer to him, and the feel of his powerful heartbeat excites me. I soon find myself hungry for so much more than just a kiss. The passion soon gets hotter and I feel my body come alive in his arms while I begin to unbutton his shirt. The feel of his massive, hard bulge pressing into me makes me even more aroused and wetter.

"Take me here and now!" I say, breathing deeply.

Tearing my thin shirt off and lifting my skirt, he wraps my legs around his waist and throws me up against the wall. I feel his enormous cock ram into me. I cry out in pleasure. Driving his cock deeper and harder with each thrust, I dig my claws into his back as he lets out a low growl, biting into my neck. His fangs pierce my soft flesh while my succubus side takes over, feeding off of his sexual essence. Hungrily, he licks the blood that flows down my neck as he takes me higher and higher in ecstasy.

I forget about everything, and I am lost in a world where it is just he and I. The feel of his hot vampiric venom running through my veins sets me on fire as I crave more and more. Turning my head, I let out a passionate cry while he continued to feed off of me.

Fuck! This is just what I need, and my mother knew it. The woman always knows before I do and points me in the right direction. This feels so fucking good and God forgive me for forgetting about my beloved Roberto but I need something to take the edge off and feed my succubus.

And Detective Erikson knows it.

Hell, I can see it deep in his eyes. I'm dripping wet and throbbing, hungry for more. He continues pounding into my womb, taking all he can get and giving me everything he has. We feed off of each other and come together over and over. I want to devour him alive and I can tell he wants to devour me and then some.

Pulling away, I look into his vampiric eyes and I'm mesmerized by how beautiful they are. He has hypnotic eyes that hold me in his stare as he looks back at me. His eyes are filled with such intense hunger that makes me shiver yet at the same time excite me, making me squirt all over his massive, hard cock like an erupting volcano. It's dangerous yet so fucking sexy.

Even as he is fucking me, I ache for him and ache badly. I can't get enough of him and he can't get enough of me. We feed and feed off of one another until we can't go any more. Breathing heavily, we collapse in one another's arms. Our bodies are covered in sweat.

"You have such an effect on me that no other woman has ever had before. There's something unique about you that has me addicted to you; not just sexually but so much more," he says.

"It might be my succubus side that you're so drawn to. She has that effect on many lovers."

"And she is so delicious."

He smiles mischievously as he lowers his head to lick my neck, making me purr with desire. I giggle as the feel of his tongue on my neck tickles my senses. Giving in to him, I turn my head to kiss him hungrily. Our tongues entwine with each other, his tongue claiming my mouth as he deepens the kiss again. I moan, hungry for much more. The flames of passion flicker brightly, craving more fuel. As the day turns to night, we continue our passionate lovemaking into the early morning hours.

Suddenly, I hear the vibration of my cell phone. I answer it and say, "Hello?" wondering who could be calling at such an hour.

Fear threatens to paralyze me—has something happened to my children or mother? But it is not them. In fact, it's someone I never thought I would hear from ever again...

Melora Stevenson.

CHAPTER 17

Eva

"I need to talk to you and Miyako immediately. How soon can you two be at the office?"

"We can be there at nine o'clock. What's going on, Melora?! We identified your dead body four weeks ago! We thought you were dead!"

A million things run across my mind. I knew Melora was a vampire and had known from the very first time we met. Miyako never even suspected. Melora knew I knew and even knew about me being a succubus but never asked about it. Something told me I could trust her with such a secret as she could trust me.

"I will explain everything when I see you both at the office. Right now, I am not in a good place to talk, nor can I say more. Just trust me on this!" Melora said, and then the call ended.

~

MIYAKO and I sit at our desks, waiting for Melora.

"How is she alive?" Miyako asks, looking at me with a raised eyebrow. "Was she alive all along?"

"I honestly don't know, Miyako, but she said she'll explain everything when she gets here."

Just then, Melora walks through the doors. She looks as if she stepped off of the pages of a high fashion magazine, hot off the press.

"Good morning, lovelies," she says with a mischievous smile, taking her glasses off to reveal her gorgeous emerald green eyes.

Miyako and I get up and run over to her, hugging her tightly with tears in our eyes. Despite our differences and Melora being such a fucking cunt, we still have love for her. We have been through so much that always brought us much closer.

"Melora! What the fuck?! You're supposed to be dead!" Miyako says.

"That wasn't me..."

Melora takes a seat at her desk as Miyako and I sit on her desk, looking at her incredulously.

"What the fuck do you mean?" I ask, confused.

"That was my twin sister, Millenia. The hunters got to her, thinking she was me, but I wasn't even in town that night. Millenia was undercover, hoping to trap the hunters and avenge our parents' deaths. The hunters have been after us for some time now. You see, I come from a royal vampire bloodline, and I am next in line for the throne. My cousin, Illenia, hired hunters to kill me so she'll be next in line for the throne. But even with me out of the picture, she has to get through to my twin sister, which means she is still out there trying to kill me, only now she thinks I'm Millenia. I only learned of this when she killed Millenia. Her brother, Gustoff, came to me that morning with this news and told me to stay low. I went back to my homeland, Transylvania. Gustoff and I devised a plan that would not only get the hunters off of my back but also kill Illenia. Illenia is responsible for the murder of Roberto, Eva."

"Wait... why would she want him dead?" I ask, tearing up at hearing this.

"They were having a secret affair for the past few years. He promised he would leave you for her but when you two began to get closer; he had a change of heart. He tried to end things with her to focus on his marriage with you and your family but she did not take it kindly. As you can see, she had your husband killed for betraying her."

"That fucking cunt!" Miyako hisses.

"Yes, Illenia is very evil. Much worse than me," Melora agrees.

One thing about Melora, she knows she's a fucking bitch and owns up to it every chance she gets.

"So, how are we going to do this? What's the plan?" I ask. I want more than ever to avenge Roberto's death and I'm willing to do whatever it takes.

"Surely you two are planning to tell Detective Hunter and Detective Erikson about this, right? We can't just do this on our own," Miyako says, being the voice of reason.

"We cannot involve the police. If we do, more innocents could die. Illenia is ruthless," Melora says.

"Why not?! This is criminal on so many levels!" Miyako says.

"For one, none of us are normal mortals. How are you going to explain *that* to the police?" Melora asks.

"Shit, this is true. No, we cannot go to the police, but we can involve Detective Erikson. He's a vampire and will know what to do." I feel bad for divulging Detective Erikson's secret to them. It's none of their business, but since Melora and I aren't human, I figure it's safe.

"You don't have to worry about me. I know all about keeping such things hidden from the mortal world," Melora says.

"Umm, since we're on the subject of Supernaturals, I have a little secret of my own, but I'm not ready to tell any of you yet. I'm not even sure of some stuff myself," Miyako says.

I look at her suspiciously. I already know her little secret—she's a witch. She hasn't come to terms with her true nature, nor has she accepted the fact.

"Okay, since Detective Erikson is a vampire, then yes, bring him in. We need someone who is on the law enforcement side for sure. His being a vampire is even better. He knows the vampire law. We have to be extremely careful as my family is royalty, and I cannot do anything that will disgrace, nor bring shame onto them. We are the alphas of the vampire world," Melora explains.

"There's just one thing that bothers me about this entire

situation..." Miyako looks at Melora with rage in her eyes. "How come you're just now coming forward with all this information? Why did you not come forward sooner?"

I feel the rage boiling deep in her; all the anger she's held back is now threatening to explode out of her like an erupting volcano.

"It was too risky. Illenia and the hunters were watching the office and you all. I had to disappear for a few weeks before coming back to explain. I couldn't put either of you at risk, and it looks like I may have. If she had Roberto killed, that means she's about to start killing you two off, starting with your families and loved ones."

"But still, you could have sent some kind of message to alert us of this danger. But as always, you only thought of yourself and your well-being and the hell with Eva and me. Tell you the truth, I feel as if there's more to this story you're not telling us," Miyako says.

Melora sits on her desk in between Miyako and me, crossing her legs, then confesses, "You're right, Miyako. There is, in fact, more to this, but right now, I cannot tell you. It is not safe."

"That is fucking bullshit! You either tell us now or we're going straight to the police! The hell with our true natures and Supernatural rules! I'm not letting you get away so easily!"

I don't know what's going on but usually, when Miyako is on to someone like this, she's dead-on. I look at Melora suspiciously and ask, "What is it you're not telling us?"

Melora looks at me with hesitation in her eyes and I see fear. "What are you so afraid of?" I ask.

"Illenia is Miyako's biological mother," Melora blurts out.

"What the fuck?!" Miyako says, then asks, "How do you know?"

"Your father was a warlord, a warlock who raped Illenia, and you were the result of the rape. You are Illenia's dirty little secret, which is why she wishes to get rid of you. She almost aborted you but for some reason, she could not bring herself to terminate your life. Instead, she gave you to a young couple from Japan who raised you as if you were their own. She trusted them to care for you and make sure you received nothing but the best of the best."

"How do you know all of this?" I ask.

"It is our family's dark secret. Illenia brought shame to our family.

The warlock who raped her was her betrothed until she killed him on their wedding night," Melora says.

"You mean I am a vampire?" Miyako asks in disbelief.

"Your half vampire and half witch," Melora confirms.

Miyako looks at me with tears in her eyes, realization suddenly hitting her, and she says, "That explains so much."

I know exactly what she's talking about. Miyako has always been unsure of who she is. She often has weird dreams that are more like visions she can never explain. She sometimes exhibits vampiric behavior, and even I suspected she might have been a vampire but there was always something that never felt right or added up.

"Eva, there's something else you do not know. Illenia is pregnant with Roberto's child. This was why she killed him. She wanted him for herself but when he rejected her and their baby, she snapped and murdered him," Melora says.

Hearing this breaks my heart into a million pieces and I fall apart. I can't believe it. Miyako holds me close and comforts me while Melora watches. If I didn't know better, it seems as if Melora dropped these bombs as a way to hurt Miyako and me. I can't help but wonder if what she's said is true and if she's the one behind all of this and not her cousin, Illenia.

I'll soon find out with the help of Detective Erikson, who will expose the real truth here.

CHAPTER 18

Miyako

I'm standing here, listening to all this shit that Melora is dumping on us and there is a rage slowly building inside me. I don't know what to make of it, I just know it demands to make itself known. Before I know what I'm doing, my eyes roll in the back of my head and I begin to float.

I feel anger radiating off my body, and I know I need to calm down before I do something stupid that I have absolutely no control over. I take deep breaths in and out, repeatedly until my feet have touched the ground and my eyes are back to normal.

"Clearly, I need to get a handle on this witch thing. As for all this other shit we've got going on, I don't know what to say. The first recollection I have of my mother is that she actually loved me, but now, Melora, you're telling me my mother wanted me dead? That makes no sense at all. I haven't told either of you yet, but *all* my memories came back. Therefore, how do I know you speak the truth?"

I'm so angry right now; I could set this whole place on fire. If Melora keeps trying me, that's exactly what the fuck I'm going to do. I'm so sick of people always shutting me out. I didn't ask for any of this. Not me being a hybrid and certainly not anyone being murdered on my account. This is all too much, and I'm just about ready to walk away from it all. As usual, Eva is the one to try and reason with me.

"Miyako, trust me, I know what you mean. I'm having a hard time believing all this shit Melora is telling us. It's too much damn drama, but unfortunately, we can't escape it no matter how hard we try. So the only thing for us to do is come up with a solution to fix this big-ass problem we have found ourselves in."

I look between them and slowly my anger dissipates. I'm still mad as hell at Melora for dying—but not really dying—on us, but I'm even madder my mother was the cause of all this. How can the first memory I have about her display such a caring, loving, and nurturing individual but then I'm told what a monster she is? I don't know what the fuck to believe, and I'm getting fed up with it all.

"Eva, I trust *you*. I know you wouldn't lead me astray. So, what will the plan be? I suggest we call Detective Hunter and Erikson as well as the tech guy that installed my security system," I tell them. They look at me as if I grew a third head or something. "What the hell are you looking at?"

"Why would you call the technician who installed your house alarm?" Melora asks.

"That's none of your business, really. I don't mean to have an attitude, but I just can't believe all the words coming out of your mouth. Eva, can I talk to you for a minute... over here please?" I ask quietly.

Eva and I walk away from Melora because I don't want her to hear what I have to say.

"What is it, Miyako?" Eva asks.

"I can tell from the look on your face that you don't believe her completely. How do we know she's telling the truth? I mean, I know I don't remember my mother, just memories of her, so I have no idea what she looks like. But how can she know this?" I ask, bewildered.

"Yeah, you're right; I don't fully trust what she says. But we also can't forget Melora is a vampire. She has been around way longer than the both of us, so the fact that she knows shit like this isn't unusual," Eva says.

"All right, we'll take that into consideration," I say as I walk us back over to where Melora is standing. "Okay, Melora, let's say we buy into all this shit you're telling us. What's the end game or the outcome of this whole situation?"

"Why don't we get everyone that's a part of this to a secure location so we can figure all that out. I've told you all I need to say. Now it's up to us to take in everything that's happened so far and all the things that could still go wrong and do something about it," Melora says.

"I'll give Julius a call, and we can all meet up at my place." I whip out my phone, dialing Julius's number.

"Are you okay? What's going on? Where are you?" he asks frantically.

"Whoa there, tiger. Slow down and take a deep breath," I say, laughing.

"I'm sorry, but you made me worried. I need to know you're okay," he demands.

"I'm okay. Eva and I are at the office. There has been a sudden turn of events that we need to fill you and Detective Erikson in on. Can both of y'all meet us at my place in about twenty minutes?"

"That shouldn't be a problem. I'll call Carl and make sure he'll be ready when I pull up and then we'll be on our way. Are you sure you're all right, *l'amour*?" he whispers.

Turning away from Eva and Melora, I whisper, "Yes, I'm okay, but something has happened that has my head all messed up. I've also found out more about my past, which explains some things, but I'm still in the dark about most of it. Once we fill you guys in, I'll have to visit Auntie Em again. She'll know what to do."

He grunts. "That doesn't say much, but you sound as if everything is okay for now. I'm only a phone call away should you need me faster than twenty minutes."

"I'll be fine. We should already be at my place once you guys get there, so I will see you then."

"Okay, babe, I'll see you in a few." He disconnects the call.

I turn back to Eva and Melora, who are both watching me intently.

"Why are y'all looking at me like that? Scared I'll cast a spell on you?" I giggle, pointing my index finger in their direction.

"Bitch, put that thing away before you hurt someone!" Melora shouts.

I look at my finger and then back at them and burst out laughing.

"Girl, you should have seen your face. As if I can cast a spell using just my finger. Get the fuck outta here!" I say, crying tears from laughing so hard.

"It's not funny. You really can do damage just using your finger. You're more powerful than you know," Melora says with a serious look on her face.

"Right, anyways... The guys will meet us at my place in twenty minutes to discuss the plan. Although, I have no idea what the plan is. After our business there, I'm going to go see Auntie Em again. I need some time alone to process all of this," I confess.

"Understandable," Melora agrees.

"Miyako, do you think it's safe for you to go back there? I mean, she lives in the middle of bum-fuck Egypt. Plus, your murdering pregnant mother is on the loose and you don't know how to use your powers, which means you can't defend yourself for shit. Are you sure that's a good idea?" Eva asks.

I know she is concerned for me, but I need to get away from all this shit before I combust.

"I'm sure, Eva, and thank you for caring. I'll be fine because Julius will be with me. Auntie can handle her own. Melora, nothing against you at all. You know I still love your bitch ass even with all this going on and the doubt that rests in the back of my mind. It's us three 'til the end, right? I just hope that the end comes no time soon," I tell them with a shaky laugh and a skeptical look in my eyes.

I don't know what will happen in the future, but with Auntie Em, Julius, Eva, Carl, and Melora on my side... What could go wrong?

CHAPTER 19

Eva

Once we get done filling Detective Hunter and Detective Erikson in on everything that recently transpired, they eye Melora suspiciously. I can already tell right off the bat that they're not taking the bait. I don't say anything, but I sense something is up.

Detective Erikson looks at me. *We need to talk immediately but not with Melora around. I know the real truth here,* he says to me telepathically.

What's wrong? I ask nervously.

Not now, not here. Melora might read minds so we must get rid of her and I'll tell you everything. In fact, I need to call someone and have them meet us here. This person knows exactly what's going on and will tell you what you need to know. Especially Miyako, he replies.

"Melora, this is all too much for us all to take in tonight. I know I said we would discuss a plan to take down Illenia but so much has happened tonight. We need to process all of this and get a good night's rest. Do you mind if we meet back at the office first thing in the morning?" I ask.

"Yes, of course. I totally understand. But we must meet first thing in the morning before it is too late."

"What do you mean?" Detective Erikson asks, looking at her intently.

"I just mean that we need to get rid of Illenia sooner rather than later. She's already on to us and once she finds me, she'll kill me and anyone else who knows of her evil plan," Melora says.

"You need not worry about Eva and Miyako. We'll take good care of them. The only one you should be worrying about is you," Detective Erikson says.

"What do you mean?" Melora asked.

"Let's just say, I'm on to you, and I know the real truth," Detective Erikson said.

Melora shifts uneasily under his gaze and gathers her things. "I'll see you both first thing in the morning. Eva, tell Miyako I said I'm sorry for unloading so much on her." Melora walks out the front door.

Miyako comes back to the room moments after Melora leaves. "Where did Melora go?" she asks.

"I asked her to leave and told her we will meet her first thing in the morning at the office."

Miyako takes a seat next to Detective Hunter and holds his hands. "Good. I'm glad she left. Auntie Em told me some things that contradict everything Melora said, especially regarding my biological mother."

"I know someone who knows Melora. She can verify everything that Melora said is a lie. The only true thing is the fact that her cousin Illenia is Miyako's birth mother," Detective Erikson says.

A few moments later, someone knocks on the door, and Miyako answers it. On the other side is a woman who closely resembles Miyako, only taller and more slender.

"Who are you?" Miyako asks.

"I am Illenia Romanoff," the woman said.

"Please let her in, Miyako. Illenia is my sire," Detective Erikson says.

"I'm not letting someone who is supposedly trying to kill me into my home!" Miyako yells.

"Trust me on this; she's not out to kill you. You got the wrong person," Detective Erikson says.

Miyako looks at Illenia, who looks at Miyako with a look of yearning and warm love deep in her eyes, "My beautiful baby girl, how you have grown into a gorgeous woman," she says, wiping a tear from her eye.

Reluctantly, Miyako allows her to enter. Illenia joins Detective Erikson on the couch and says, "Melora has lied to you about me and my intentions. I would never do anything to harm or hurt my baby girl. Melora is the one who is out to kill you and also, I am not the one who had an affair with Roberto, nor am I pregnant by him. Melora is the one who had an affair with Roberto and killed him for rejecting her and their baby."

I don't know this woman but something rings true in what she's said. I always knew Melora wanted Roberto for herself but I never thought she would get pregnant by him, nor would I even imagine her killing him.

"There's more," Detective Erikson says. "Melora was the one who killed her identical twin, Millenia. The real truth of the matter is Melora wanted to be next in line for the throne. She always envied Millenia because she was the good and dutiful twin. Everyone loved, adored, and respected Millenia. Melora couldn't stand it and decided to kill her and make it look as if it was her."

"Auntie Em pretty much confirmed the same thing. Although she never told me about Illenia being my biological mother, she did say my biological mother loved me truly and dearly. That she would never do anything to hurt me. I knew Melora was lying, I knew it was just too fucking crazy to be true," Miyako said.

"So, what do we do?" I ask.

"We catch her in a lie, and then we take her down," Detective Hunter says. "With Illenia here, we can set her up and then bring out Illenia, who will expose her for the killer that she is. Once she is exposed, we can take her in and put her on trial. No doubt she will be found guilty and executed. We have a special Supernatural council that handles crimes within the immortal and Supernatural realm. Tomorrow morning before you meet with her, we will wire you both so that we can hear everything. We need to get her to confess to her crimes, and then we will step in and arrest her. We will also bring Illenia with us, who will confront her and expose her to us all. Without her confession, we have nothing."

"Can you two handle this?" Detective Hunter asks, looking at Miyako.

"Oh, hell yeah! She will get what she so rightly deserves! Karma's a bitch when you fuck with her!" Miyako says.

"I definitely can handle this. It's time she gets a dose of her own medicine. Especially after she murdered my beloved Roberto," I add.

CHAPTER 20

Miyako

We all take our leave. My mother rides with me and Julius back to his place. I have a ton of questions, and I know she does, too. Leave it to Julius to break the silence we have going on.

He clears his throat, turning slightly while his eyes are still on the road, and starts up a conversation.

"So, Illenia, how sure are you that this plan will work? Melora sounds like a hell of a woman scorned and out for more than just blood."

"Well, you forget the fact that I am a powerful vampire and my daughter is one of the most powerful witches in the world, even though she has yet to master her powers. When she does, everyone should watch out." She laughs, leaning up and placing her hand on my shoulder.

Reaching back, I turn and place mine on top of hers. I can tell my mother is nervous, but also proud of me. Even though we've been apart for so long, it seems like she never stopped loving me. This leads to my next question.

"Is it true what Melora said about my father?" I ask.

"He was most definitely a warlock but no, he did not rape me. We were in love. We were on the run, him and me, because neither my coven nor his approved of our union. So rather than give everyone else what they wanted, we decided to do what was best for us. Then you came along and changed it all. There has never been a hybrid as powerful as you, my darling girl."

"I don't get it. Why am I so special? I don't even have vampiric traits or witchy skills. I mean, I've seen my memories and know what happened, but if I was forced to not remember it all, how can I be a threat to anyone? This just doesn't make sense and has me so messed up in the head! Where is my father now? Is my dad okay?" I ask with shaky words.

"Baby, I'm not sure what happened to your father," she says, letting my hand go, and resting back in her seat. "He was taken from me years ago, shortly after I gave you to your foster mom and dad. I knew you would be okay with them, so I went on a manhunt to find my Luis. I'm so close I can taste it, but when Detective Erikson followed all the signs that pointed to me and told me about the trouble you were in, I had to reveal myself."

"Were you close to finding him before you were pulled away?" I ask with hope.

"So close, baby, so close that I can feel him, right here." She places her hand over her heart.

Before I know it, we pull up to Julius's house. Shutting off the car, he walks over to my mother's door and helps her out. Once she's settled, he comes and opens my door and helps me out also.

"Thanks for being there for me tonight, with all this shit going on," I say, waving my hand back and forth.

"There's nowhere else I'd rather be, *l'amour*," he says, placing a gentle kiss on my lips.

"You two make a beautiful couple, darling," my mother tells me.

"Thank you. We should probably go inside. We don't want to get caught in some more shit we won't be able to get ourselves out of," I tell them.

"Maybe you should call Auntie to come and put some wards on the house, unless you know how to do that?" Mom asks me.

"No, I haven't practiced any spells yet. I just know my emotions affect the weather," I explain to her as we walk to the front door while Julius goes inside and does a quick sweep of the place.

"Oh, I know all about that, dear," Mom says with a laugh.

"How do you know?" I ask with a bewildered look on my face.

She winks. "Even though you didn't see me doesn't mean I was never around."

"Interesting. Let me call Auntie to see if she can come over or tell me how to put up some protection spells here and at Eva's. I'll be right back."

I leave my mom and Julius in the living room.

"Do you love my daughter?" I hear her ask Julius. Just as I'm about to go back in and rip her a new one, he answers.

"Forgive me, ma'am, for how I answer that question, but yes, I fucking love her with all my heart. I know we moved fast, but that doesn't matter to me. I think I fell for her the first time we met."

My heart melts like lava. Then, something else hits me... I'm in Julius's room, which is on the other side of the house, so how the fuck did I just hear that?

"Because, chile, you're half vampire, of course."

I yelp in surprise as Auntie Em materializes out of thin air.

"How the hell did you do that? You scared the living shit out of me, Auntie!" I shout.

I hear pounding footsteps. Julius has shifted into his wolf form and my mother's eyes have changed to red and her teeth protrude from her gums.

"Jeez, people, ready to kill much?" I giggle.

"Baby, we heard you scream, so of course, we came running. Although, I was very surprised when Julius's clothes began to rip and he changed before my eyes. I should have known he was a shifter, but your scent was also on him, causing me to miss it."

She has a twinkle in her eye. I see where I get this hopeless romantic shit from. I look down at the floor, blushing.

"Mom, stop making this weird."

"Oh, bother!" she says, tears falling from her eyes.

"What's wrong? Why are you crying?"

She wraps her arms around me. "Because, sweetie, you called me mom."

"I suppose I did. Well, we have work to do... Mom. Auntie scared the crap out of me and I just realized my hearing is top-notch now," I say, looking at Julius with lust in my eyes as he stands in his birthday suit.

Auntie quickly throws him a towel that I have no idea where she got from. I need this man tonight, and I don't care if my mother is in the house or not. I will get my way.

"Dear, the wards are done. I will pop over to Eva's and do the same there. Illenia, honey, would you like to come with me?" she asks with a hint of mischief.

"I suppose I would love to. Give these kids time to process what all happened here today. My darling girl, I will be back within an hour or two. I'm in good hands and so are you. Get some sleep; we will be back before you know it." She pulls me in for a hug, which I gladly give in return.

"Okay, Mom. Auntie, I'll see y'all in a few. I'll text Eva to let her know y'all are on the way," I say, whipping out my phone and sending Eva a quick text.

My mom and Auntie are coming over to put wards up around your house. Let them know if they need to do the same to Carl's. Love you, goodnight and see you in the morning.

Eva responds:

Thanks, bitch. See you in the morning. You better get some sleep and no dick!

I can see her laughing through the phone. I turn back around to tell them Eva is ready but Auntie grabs Mom's hands and they both vanish.

They didn't even bother using the front door. I'm going to have to learn that nifty trick.

"Come here, *l'amour*," Julius beckons me to him. I happily oblige. "I have you to myself for the next two hours, and I plan on worshiping your body like the goddess you are tonight."

"Did you mean what you told my mother back there?" I ask, bending my head to try and shield my face from him.

"You know I did, *l'amour*. You've known all along how I've felt. I think I've loved you since the first day we met," he confesses.

"I love you too, Julius. Take me upstairs and show me all the ways you love me before my mother and auntie come back," I purr to him.

"Your wish is my command."

He lifts me in his arms and carts me off to his bed. Boy, does he make good on his promises. We make love into the night.

I hear my mom and Auntie come back to Julius's within two hours of them leaving, but I'm too tired to do anything but sleep in Julius's arms. This is exactly what I need before our big day tomorrow. I'm scared shitless, but dammit, I'll use what I got to make sure we all come out on top of all this.

CHAPTER 21

Eva

Early the next morning, Miyako and Detective Hunter come over to my place. Detective Erikson is already here since he spent the night with me.

Miyako and I watch as Detective Hunter and Detective Erikson meticulously place wires all over our bodies, making sure they're not visible. I look over at Miyako, who's quite enjoying Detective Hunter's hands all over her nearly naked body. Hearing her giggle and laugh warms my heart, just knowing that she is back to her old cheerful self despite all that has recently transpired and the fact that we're about to take Melora down in a matter of hours. I look down at Detective Erikson, who's watching me with those gorgeous eyes of his, filled with such warmth and love. I smile at him and touched his hand.

Miyako looks at me. She smiles nervously. I reach out and grab her hand, giving it a tiny squeeze. "Are you okay?"

Miyako squeezes my hand in return and then says, "I am more than okay. I finally got to meet my mother, and we're reconnecting on so many levels. I feel complete, as if I am 100% whole. Although it was under such circumstances, it was a true genuine blessing in disguise. I am truly blessed and thankful to have her back in my life."

I can't help but get teary-eyed. "You deserve the best hun, you truly do."

"All right, we're set to go," Detective Erikson says as he stands and dusts himself off. "You almost done, Julius?" He has a look of mischievousness in his eyes as if he knows what is keeping his partner.

Detective Hunter wears an all-knowing, mischievous smile of his own and says, "Just about. I got a bit distracted, but we're all set over here. Just double-checking some stuff but other than that she is ready to go."

We head to my black Cadillac Escalade parked out back. Detective Erikson and Detective Hunter carry a couple of huge duffle bags that look pretty heavy, filled with guns and other weapons no doubt. I open the back for them so that they can put their bags in the back. Once they're done, Detective Hunter gets in the back seat with Miyako while Detective Erikson walks over to the driver's side. I slide over to the passenger seat so that he can take the driver's seat.

We make a pit stop at Dunkin' Donuts to grab some hot coffee. We will need all the caffeine we can get for what we're about to do today. It's a silent ride to the office as we all mentally prepare for the huge task ahead of us. It's up to Miyako and me to get Melora to confess to her crimes. We have to be careful and creative in how we go about it. I know Melora better, and I know just what to say to make her crack.

One of her biggest weaknesses is my close relationship with Miyako. She's always envied Miyako for being so close to me. Melora can't stand it. If Melora had a chance, she would destroy mine and Miyako's friendship just so she could replace Miyako. And she has tried, many times, but always failed. Miyako and I have a sisterly bond that no one can destroy. Miyako is Melora's kryptonite. And I'm about to use Miyako as a weapon against Melora for the greater good.

By the time we reach the office, Melora is already there. I don't know what it is, but the room suddenly grows unusually colder. Something is not right, something is very wrong here. Melora has that fake-ass bitch smile on her face, the same smile she always wears anytime she's up to no good. I suddenly feel as if shit is about to go down at any moment. Melora's vampiric eyes now show dark, bloody-red and the tips of her fangs are visible.

"Good morning, Melora," I say.

"Good morning, Eva," she replies.

Miyako says nothing as she walks over to her desk and takes a seat. Following in her footsteps, I walk over to my desk and have a seat. Melora sits on her desk, watching us with that sinister smile and dark, intent red glowing eyes.

"I see you two have been busy since we parted ways last night," Melora says.

"We have. In fact, we learned a thing or two," I say calmly.

"What have you learned?" she asks.

"I think you already know."

She blinks as if innocent. "How would I know anything other than what I disclosed to you both yesterday?"

"Now you know that's a damn lie!" Miyako says, deep rage burning in her eyes.

Knowing her emotions are connected to her witch powers, I walk over to her desk and touch her hand softly. Sending soothing sensations throughout her body with my touch alone, she calms down.

"Are you talking about the fact that Miyako is a powerful witch and vampire hybrid? Or the fact that you know the truth about Illenia not being out to kill her? Or did you learn the *real* truth about Roberto's death, Eva?" Melora teases.

"What is the real truth about Roberto's death?" I ask, suddenly forgetting the plan and ready to rip her head off.

"Roberto and I were secretly married long before he ever laid eyes on you. But since it was forbidden for our kind to intermingle with his, the marriage was annulled. But what he didn't know, what no one knew, was that I gave birth to his first daughter. She's even more powerful than Miyako!" Melora says, laughing wickedly.

I'm filled with rage and hurt. Before I realize what I'm doing, I find myself on top of her with my hands wrapped around her neck in a vise grip, choking the life from her.

"You vile, wretched creature!" I hiss. "You've always been envious of what others have because you know deep down you will never be genuinely happy as everyone else. You knew you could never find a man as good as my Roberto. The real truth of the matter had nothing to do with you two being forbidden from being together. Roberto and I knew each other long before our college years. Our union was blessed by the elders, and we were destined to be together from our births. Think as you like, but you never had a chance with him to begin with. As for this love child of yours, Roberto knew all about it and confessed it wasn't his. He would have sensed it ages ago!" I say, my grip around her neck growing tighter.

Miyako tries to pull me off of Melora, saying, "Eva! Get off of her! She's only egging you on! You know this!"

Hearing her makes me realize what's happening and I let go of Melora and get up. I stand over her, watching her cough and catch her breath. She's unaffected and laughs my attack off.

"Cut the bullshit, Melora! Admit it was you who killed your twin sister and Roberto!" Miyako says.

Melora didn't see that coming, and rage fills her eyes.

"How did you know?" she asks, looking at Miyako.

"We have our ways of finding out. Your scent was all over their dead bodies as well as your fingerprints. Did you really think we would fall for those nasty, vicious lies of yours?" I ask. "You forget who you're dealing with. I know you better than anyone else, and I knew right from the beginning you were lying about everything. I just want to hear it from your mouth and what the true reasons behind your actions are."

"You were right about one thing, I always desired Roberto. I always envied you because he chose you over me. I envied you because he chose you to have a family with. As for my twin sister, I envied the fact she was next in line for the throne, which is *my* true birthright. I was the oldest, but no one knew. She was the most loved and respected while I was viewed as the vicious bitch that should have never been born," Melora says angrily.

The door bursts open with Detective Erikson, Detective Hunter, along with Illenia following close behind them.

Detective Erikson walks over to Melora and says, "Ms. Melora Stevenson, you are hereby under arrest. You will now stand trial before the council for your crimes against your kind."

Detective Hunter slaps sterling silver handcuffs on Melora's wrists.

The sizzling sound coming from her skin where the silver touches it is all I need to hear to know she'll get what she so rightly deserves in the end.

"Did you think you could turn my flesh and blood against me, cousin?" Illenia asks as she walks right up to Melora, looking her dead in the eye.

"It's not my fault you were such a coward. You were so afraid of your own daughter, who was far more powerful than you ever will be," Melora said.

"I pray you meet true death so that you can never ruin anyone else's life ever again. You have always been a wretched, miserable creature, out to destroy true beauty and happiness," Illenia says. "You are a disgrace to the family, and you should have been destroyed when you were born into darkness."

Two Weeks Later...

Melora finally received what she so rightly deserved. A week ago, she met death when she was executed by decapitation. Her head hangs in the dungeons of the elders.

For the very first time in a very long time, I feel at peace. I feel as if Roberto's death has been avenged and so much more. Miyako is engaged to Detective Hunter. Miyako's mother lives with Auntie Em. Illenia and Auntie Em are teaching Miyako how to use her magic and master it.

Detective Erikson and I are officially together. Taking things nice and slow. I've never been so happy or so at peace. My children view him as a second father, which makes me smile as he will someday be their stepfather.

"How are you, my beautiful goddess?" he asks, kissing me softly.

"I'm just blessed to have you in my life. I am finally truly happy," I reply, kissing him back.

CHAPTER 22

Miyako

After all that's happened these last two weeks, I'm finally at peace. Thinking back to our showdown with Melora on that fateful day, I thought she would put up more of a fight and I would have gotten to unleash my true self on her. But she didn't and that was a big disappointment, but it was really for the best. Who knows what could have happened? Since I haven't mastered powers yet, I could have killed us all. I laugh to myself at my stupidity. Now, Melora is gone forever and can't wreak havoc and mayhem on anyone else's lives. I couldn't be happier.

Eva and I have grown much closer without Melora in our way, I think as we take a walk in the park while the kids are playing.

"Eva, have I ever told you how much I love you and value our friendship?" I ask her, squeezing her hand tightly in mine.

"Look here, bitch, stop getting all mushy on me." She laughs. "I know just how much you love me because the feeling is mutual."

"I know, but with all that's happened, I just feel the need to say it now and again. So, get used to it," I tell her.

"I'll never get used to it," she confesses while rolling her eyes with the hint of a smile on her lips.

"Yeah, you will. We see each other almost every single day, not to mention the planning of the wedding coming up soon. But the real question is, when will you and Carl talk about tying the knot?"

"Um, slow your roll. We're taking things one day at a time. I'm sure it will happen one day but no time soon."

"I respect that. Looks like the guys are having a blast with the kids, but Julius and I will soon head out. My mom and Auntie Em said they had something important they want to discuss with me," I inform her.

"Okay. Well, keep me posted, bitch." She laughs, pulling me into a hug.

I giggle. "And you know I will. Let me give the babies a hug and a kiss before we go."

After Julius and I say our goodbyes, we head over to Auntie Em's house. On the way there, I can't help but think how life couldn't be any better for me. My mother is in the picture, I have the man of my dreams with me every step of the way, and I'm learning to master my powers. Everything is going my way.

Suddenly, I'm hit with a powerful wave of nausea that hits me like a ton of bricks.

"Julius, pull over. I'm going to be sick!" I yell, grabbing my mouth as he swerves to the side of the road.

As soon as the car stops, I fling the door open and everything I ate this morning comes up.

"*L'amour*, what's wrong?" he asks, standing by me with a concerned look.

"I don't know. I just felt sick to my stomach all of a sudden. Must have been something I ate paired with the heat of the day. I'm okay now," I tell him as I lean back in my seat.

He looks at me like he isn't buying it but rounds back to the driver's side and we take off again. We arrive at Auntie's house in no time. As always, the door opens before we have a chance to knock.

"We are out back, dears," I hear Auntie call.

"What on earth are y'all doing back there?" I ask them as we walk around the clothesline filled with clothes.

I see Auntie Em and Mom near the garden with a man.

"Interesting. I didn't know Mom had any other friends besides Auntie, let alone a male friend," I say in bewilderment.

But when the man turns around, I'm hit with a sense of familiarity. I don't know where or how I could know this man, but I feel as if I do.

"It's because you do, dear," Auntie Em says to me as she comes to stand near me. Mom turns around then. She and her mystery man walk over to where Julius and I stand.

"Hey, everyone, what's going on?" I ask with a shaky voice.

"Baby, I have some exciting news. You see, I never gave up on looking for your father. Not ever. Now, I know you don't remember him, but—"

She doesn't get to finish her sentence before I speak to the man in question.

"Papa? Is it really you?" I ask as tears begin streaming down my face.

"Oh, my sweet princess, it's me," he says as he picks me up in a full embrace.

"I can't believe it's really you," I say, hugging him tightly, never wanting to let him go.

"It's okay, princess, it was a long time ago. Turns out, Melora was the one that had me imprisoned all this time. When she died, I was set free."

"In that case, I'm glad that bitch is gone!" I shout with glee. "Papa, I'm so glad you're here. You have to see all the things I've been learning, I have to show you my house, and... I'm engaged!" I yell, showing him my ring finger.

"I'm so proud of you, princess. Where is this mystery man that has captured my baby girl's heart?" he says, looking in Julius's direction.

Julius steps around me and extends his hand to my papa. "Hello, sir, I'm Julius Hunter, and it's a pleasure to meet you. Under normal circumstances, I would have asked you for her hand in marriage so I want to apologize about that."

"No need to apologize, son. I just got back so it's okay. As long as can walk my princess down the aisle to the man that loves her more th himself, I'm okay with that," he says, kissing my cheek.

"Stop it, Papa. You're making me blush."

"All right, dears, who's hungry?" Auntie asks.

"We are," I answer for us all.

"Well, let's all go inside and eat some of this delicious meal we've prepared for everyone," Auntie Em says.

We make our way back into the house and I'm hit with the most amazing aroma. I take a good whiff and instantly, my stomach starts churning. I run out of the kitchen and into the bathroom where I throw up water. After there is nothing left to throw up, I dry heave. There is a knock at the door.

"Pumpkin, can I come in?" Mom asks.

"Yes, Momma, please come in," I say weakly.

"What's wrong, baby? Julius says you got sick like this on the way here."

"Yeah, I did, but I thought it was just from the heat when we were at the park with Eva, Carl, and the kids. Now, I'm not so sure. Maybe it's stress from the wedding and other things," I say.

"Maybe, or maybe it could be something else," she hints with a smile.

"What do you know, Momma? Tell me!" I demand.

"Your Auntie and I think you're pregnant, but we aren't sure. Well, she's sure but won't tell me. So, when you find out, you have to share the news with us."

"But Momma, I haven't missed my period at all," I inform her.

"Maybe so, but you can have a period during your whole pregnancy in case you forgot. Just take a test when you're ready, baby," she says, helping me up and placing a kiss on my cheek.

I give what she says some thought and decide before Julius and I ' home, I'm going to buy a test. For now, we will carry on as if ˙ has happened.

˙ the bathroom, I go in search of Julius so we can all sit down ˙ce meal together.

~

˙ious, Momma and Auntie, thank you for ˙ulius and I are going to head home. I'm a bit

˙ back and get to have you in my life. Both

your mother and I are so proud of you. Son, thank you for loving my daughter and keeping her safe. Welcome to the family," he says, pulling Julius and me into a tight embrace.

"Thank you, Papa. I love you," I say.

"Thank you, sir, that means the world to me," Julius says.

"All right, you two kids get on out of here," Papa says.

Julius and I head out to the car and hop back on the road to my house.

"Before we head home, can you stop by the store for a sec? I just need to pick up a few things."

"Anything for you, baby," he says, picking up my hand and placing a kiss on it.

I settle back and close my eyes for a few. The next thing I know, we're at the store.

"Do you want me to come in with you, *l'amour*?" he asks.

"No, baby, I won't be long."

I get out of the car, go inside, and make the purchase. I get a few other things in case he asks what all I got. After paying, I slide the test inside my purse. Making it back to the car, we head home. I unlock the door and disarm the alarm.

"I'm going to shower," I announce.

"Would you like me to join?" he asks with lust-filled eyes.

"Not this time, big guy." I laugh. "I want to wash this day away alone, but I won't be long."

"Okay, hurry back to me. The night is still young, and I want to make love to my beautiful bride-to-be," he declares.

"Your wish is *my* command. I'll be out in a jiff."

Grabbing my purse, I head for the bathroom. Once inside, I lock the door and open the test. I go to the toilet and pee on the stick, and then I hop in the shower because I have to wait for the results. I take a cowboy shower because I'm anxious to see the results.

I slowly walk to the sink and grab the test. My eyes widen to the size of saucers as I see two pink lines staring back.

"Oh. My. Goodness. I'm pregnant!" I shriek.

Julius comes running to the door and starts banging on it. "Miyako, open the door! What's wrong?" he yells from the other side.

I rush to the door, fling it open, and jump into his arms. "Nothing's wrong, everything in my life is just right!" I say, placing a kiss on his lips and showing him the test.

"We're pregnant?" he asks. That question alone lets me know we are in this for the long haul... together.

"Yes, baby, we are!" I shout as he picks me up and swings me around while peppering kisses down my face. "I love you, baby."

"I love you more!"

Just like that, my life is complete. I can't wait to share the news with everyone. But for now, I'm going to enjoy the company of my man as we make love through the night.

THE END